The Rake

Other Books by Karen Lynn

MIDSUMMER MOON
DUAL DESTINY
A SCOTTISH MARRIAGE
DOUBLE MASQUERADE

The Rake

KAREN LYNN

DOUBLEDAY & COMPANY, INC.
GARDEN CITY, NEW YORK
1986

All of the characters in this book
are fictitious, and any resemblance
to actual persons, living or dead,
is purely coincidental.

Library of Congress Cataloging-in-Publication Data

Lynn, Karen.
The rake.

I. Title.
PS3562.Y4447R3   1986   813'.54   86-11575
ISBN 0-385-23566-6

For Lawrence G. Taylor with love and appreciation

Our husband, father, and grandfather, who gives us constant encouragement, solves our myriad problems, and is our second line of defense.

The Rake

CHAPTER ONE

Sharisse Satterleigh sat in the chintz-covered arm chair and stared unseeingly through the open french window. The sun, streaming through the window, highlighted several rich shades of red in the curls dangling from a knot at the back of her head. Her large brown eyes weren't focused on the panoramic view before her or on the letter she had crushed in her slender hands.

The rolling broad green lawn stretched to the hedgerows that marked the formal gardens. A myriad colors fought for supremacy, each having a set height and shape, forming neat rows and patterns around the meandering walks.

A long sigh escaped her now somber lips and a single tear trickled over a high cheekbone and made a trail down her cheek. With a toss of her head and a distinct thrust to her chin she dashed away the tear. Her entire demeanor showed a determination not known to many women of her day.

The laughing voice of a little girl wafting through the open window broke the strained silence in the drawing room. "The tarts were lovely, Françoise. I'll be glad to sample them anytime."

The scolding voice of the cook broke into volatile French as she pushed the little scamp from the open kitchen door.

Sharisse straightened out the official letter once more. The seal was impressive, proclaiming the document to be from the Commissioner at Delhi, India. The words jumped out at her.

March 17, 1819

It is with regret we wish to inform you of the death of Lieutenant Sidney Satterleigh, in a skirmish with a native hill tribe while on a routine patrol. There were no survivors of the detail. Lieutenant Satterleigh was decorated just before this incident for his courage in putting his men's safety first. He was a valiant fighter and we shall sorely miss him.

Platitudes followed with the assurance that Sidney's personal effects would be forwarded to England.

The lump in her throat made it impossible to swallow. Sidney had written several times of his uncanny ability to sniff out trouble and take appropriate action. It seemed that his luck had finally run out.

First her father, a comparatively young and healthy man, had been killed in an accident. Now her brother was gone too and she would miss him even more than she would miss her father. Sidney had always been so lighthearted, so full of fun and humor, and always her staunch supporter. They had shared so many carefree days on the estate riding to hounds and shooting. The estate wouldn't be the same without him.

Moreover, with both her father and Sidney gone, the estate would pass to the next male relative. She and Polly would be without any means of support or, for that matter, a place to live. Her father, typical of his kind, had believed that his son would see to his daughters' needs. Sharisse paled as she realized that the only income that would be forthcoming was the meager dress allowance paid to her quarterly.

"Dear Heaven," she whispered in a strangled voice, "what am I to do?" Sharisse never heard the patter of feet racing across the stone court or the door that was thrown open.

A small girl of ten in a much rumpled pinafore burst into the room, her copper pigtails bobbing up and down. Her brown eyes were alight with mischief as she ran over to her sister. She cocked her head to one side as she observed Sharisse. "Must be important to make you sit so still," she gurgled, grinning, and twitched the letter from fingers that had gone slack.

"No!" wailed Sharisse, shocked into mobility. She reached out to retrieve the revealing document, but Polly flounced off and read as she went. The child's face became a study in sobriety and she threw the letter on the floor and stamped on it. Then she flew across the room and into Sharisse's waiting arms, tears streaming down her contrite face.

Sharisse rocked Polly in her arms, her thoughts centering on the child she was comforting. She had long ago become a mother figure to the little girl and spoiled her dreadfully, trying earnestly to make up for the loss of one parent and then two. How could she manage to support the two of them? She wasn't trained for any kind of work, although she had proved that with the help of their old bailiff, Jem Starr, she could run the estates. If she could only gain a little time to look around, she might be able to find a solution.

She crooned softly to Polly as her mind flitted over various possibilities. She sorted and discarded them as if she were shuffling cards. Of a sudden, she stopped rocking Polly. What if no one knew of Sidney's death right away? If the news could be postponed even a month to begin the search for the new heir, then she would have a respite to find a more permanent solution. The only hitch in the thought was that Polly knew the truth.

"Polly?" She pushed a few strands of hair away from the child's face. "How good are you at keeping a secret? This would be one so big and important it could make a difference in our lives."

Polly stopped sniffling and looked up at the serious face of her sister. Polly could be a very determined child when she had a mind to. "If it's that important I can keep it. Is it a grown-up secret?"

The thread of excitement in the child's voice made Sharisse smile. How quickly children could be turned from one mood to another. "Do you know what it means when an estate is entailed?"

Polly snuggled down deeper in Sharisse's arms and made herself comfortable. "I've heard you speak of it, but I'm not sure what it means."

"It's a way we do things to make sure the property stays in

the family by passing it down through the male members of the family."

"Oh, you mean from father to son?"

"Yes, but in this case, Sidney has no son to leave the property to, so some distant male relative will come to live here and he won't want to be bothered with us. We have to find ourselves a new place to live."

Polly sat up abruptly. "That won't be so hard. All you have to do is to decide to marry a man who has an estate like ours." She threw her arms around her sister's neck and hugged her fiercely. "I love you, Sharisse. You're beautiful and any man would be lucky to have you."

Tears silently streamed down Sharisse's face as she returned Polly's hug. The love and trust Polly had in her helped her to make a resolve. Polly wouldn't suffer because of this tragedy. And Polly's suggestion? The thought brought a smile to her face. It was easier said than done. She felt she had been on the shelf anytime these past several years. She plainly didn't take. She was too tall, too determined, and made no push to be pleasing to gentlemen who obviously wanted a woman for her beauty and nothing else. She had told her father several times that when she found a man that reminded her of himself, she would marry him. That had been six years before and she hadn't met a man that could in any way measure up to her father.

Now she took stock of her attributes, evaluating them rather severely. She thought her height was going to be the worst handicap to overcome. Her face and figure were passable, but her unruly tongue had gotten her in trouble more times than she cared to remember. Her marriage portion would be respectable, for she knew that her father had set that in his will so there could be no haggling over it. Polly might prove a stumbling block, but her sister would come with her no matter what. She wouldn't accept any offer without considering how Polly would be received. Sharisse, at twenty-three, was past the age where she expected to feel anything more than fondness for a husband. She had relegated those dreams to her girlhood days, but the prospect of settling for less seemed a bit daunting.

Little did she realize that she was a sparkling beauty built on queenly lines and that the only reason that she had yet to receive an offer was that she held almost the entire male sex in contempt.

"The first thing we have to do is to gain a little time. I don't mean to try to do someone out of his rightful inheritance, but it can't hurt anyone to have to wait a few weeks longer to take over the Meadows. Now what I need from you is your solemn promise that you'll not tell anyone about this letter. This is the secret. Can you keep it, Elizabeth?"

Polly slid off Sharisse's lap and stood tall before her. When Sharisse called her by her real name Polly knew she was serious. The little fingers made the age-old sign of keeping a promise as she crossed her heart and raised her right hand. "I promise." Her voice trembled for a moment. "This means we won't get to see Sidney again, doesn't it?"

Sharisse nodded and took her hand. Together they retrieved the letter and Sharisse put it in the pocket of her dress. Making a great effort, Sharisse turned Polly to her and questioned with a smile, "And now, miss, tell me just what you were up to when you flew through the door? I could hear cook's voice scolding all the way in here."

Polly grinned unrepentantly and placed both hands on her hips. "Cook made some jam tartlets and they had just come out of the oven. I only snitched two." Her eyes twinkled merrily as she admitted the theft.

Sharisse had to bite her cheek to keep from smiling at the prank, remembering time upon time when she had done the same. "You mustn't make cook angry. What would we do without her?" Even as she asked the question, she knew that the future wouldn't hold cook. She would want to stay at the Meadows, since her children were scattered about the near countryside. Thinking about cook brought questions of pensions, but that would have to wait until she was ready to announce Sidney's death.

"Now, Polly, I want to be certain that you understand how important our secret is. I know someone is going to inquire about the letter I received. A foreign postmark is a tempting piece of gossip and I know that the fact will be all over the village by evening." She waited for Polly's complete attention before continuing. "I am going to say that we have received word that Sidney is gravely wounded and has been taken to a hospital in France to a noted specialist."

Polly agreed that the story had merit. "I'll remember, if anyone asks. Then she reached up and gave her sister a big hug and kiss. "Don't worry, Rissy, I'll help take care of you." With that parting shot the little girl fled the room, embarrassed at her forwardness.

Sharisse's heart swelled at the devotion of her little sister. "I won't fail you, sweetheart. I will find a solution to this tangle no matter what it takes." Her stomach turned at the thought of marrying some gentleman for his money, and she gritted her teeth. Mayhap it wouldn't come to that.

Andrew Lindley tooled his curricle down the pike to Ashford. As he flashed by, people stopped to admire the elegant driver who handled his pair of matched bays with a deal of expertise. His countenance was swarthy from long exposure to the sun, but his prominent cheekbones and blade-thin nose proclaimed him a member of the aristocracy. The gentleman couldn't be called handsome by any means, but his sparkling blue eyes were alive, dancing with exuberance, and an aura of strength radiated from him.

His face became set in stern lines as he thought of the disagreeable task that he had agreed to perform. It was certainly not one of his choosing but it was a little difficult to turn down Mr. Barton Conroy, the Commissioner at Delhi, when he asked a favor. The man had been of great assistance to him through the years in his trading ventures.

Andrew had seen a deal of himself in the adventurous lad who had been Lieutenant Satterleigh. The young man had a zest for living and making instant decisions. Moreover, the lieutenant had impressed him as being awake upon every suit and front in his business of soldiering. It was a shame to lose one who could have made so much difference in dealing with the situations as he grew older and wiser. Andrew sighed and returned his mind to the task at hand. He had a satchel of the Satterleigh's effects to present to the young man's father. The prospect of facing grieving relatives left a distinctly unpleasant taste in his mouth.

It brought back his own departure from England some seventeen years earlier after his last and most outrageous prank. His mother had sobbed, while his aunt had chafed the good woman's hands, murmuring soothing phrases. His father and uncle had joined ranks against him. They had ranted, rampaged, and lectured until they finally ran out of things to say. It was at that time that Andrew had booked a one-way passage on the steamer to India, doffed his top hat to the ladies, and wished them all well. With a kiss to his mother's cheek he had stormed out into the early-morning air and made his way to the quay.

That probably had been his salvation. He made his way up in the countinghouses of Delhi through hard work and a keen head for business. He'd saved every groat he earned and had invested it in any scheme that seemed to promise a handsome profit. He hadn't gone unrewarded. That fact alone made him feel that his time hadn't been wasted. Having made his fortune, he considered his debt to his family and society paid. He was now ready to untangle his affairs in England.

His solicitor had sent word that his father, mother, and brother had succumbed to an attack of cow fever and that he was now sole heir to the estate. The solicitor had also acknowledged the poor condition of the property and the number of debts that would have to be cleared to save the property from foreclosure.

Andrew looked fondly at the countryside he'd missed for nearly eighteen years. The summer sky was a brilliant blue with an occasional fluff of cloud floating in the air. The air smelled fresh and clean, the odor of clover filling his nostrils.

Ahead he could see the village of Ashford, and knew that the Meadows lay somewhere to the north. As he reached the dusty main street, he pulled his team to miss the small children dancing in and out of the doorways.

Andrew stopped at the small post office, looped his reins about a post, and strode into the building. A small, elderly man with pince-nez glasses perched on the very tip of his nose looked up as he opened the door.

"What ken I do fer ye, sir?"

"Can you direct me to the Meadows?"

The old man pushed his glasses up his nose and replied evenly, "Take the first turn to the left out of town." His finger pointed to the opposite end of town. "It's about four miles out." The man cocked his head. "What might be your interest in the Meadows?"

Andrew's brows came together and his eyes threw off sparks like flint. "I don't believe I said," he murmured with deceptive calm, and clamped his jaw shut. As he swung out the door he noted the startled expressions on the two elderly ladies seated on a bench. England never changed, there was always a group of tabbies to poke their noses in someone else's business.

As he tooled his pair along the dirt road that led to the Meadows, his thoughts turned to the words he might use to break the news gently to the father of the dead boy, if the post hadn't already done the job. That was one reason he'd stayed overnight at Dover. He hadn't wanted to be the advance guard on this chore. The rear guard was bad enough.

As the estate came into view he noted the even hedgerows. It took a hundred years to grow a good one. Evidently these had had some care. The permanence of England warmed his blood. He might have been away for almost a lifetime, but the country was a part of him even now. The iron gates stood open in silent invitation. A long drive was lined with massive oak trees and at the end it circled a reflecting pool that captured the large portico of the hall. The modestly large stone building attracted him with its long mullioned windows glinting in the sun. The entire scene seemed welcoming, down to the vast green lawns that stretched out on either side.

He jumped down from the carriage and looked for a place to tie the curricle. As he did he became aware of the sound of running footsteps. A smile touched his lips as he recognized the laugh of a child. Barreling around the building came a whirlwind of pinafore, pigtails, and lace. Andrew picked her up as she collided with him and set her on her feet in front of him.

"What's your hurry, little one?"

Polly looked shocked as she encountered Andrew's hard length. "Let me go!"

Just then an old voice could be heard in the distance calling, "Miss Elizabeth! Stop this instant!"

"From the look of your pinafore, I'd say that you've been snitching tarts and from your breath, I'd venture, blueberry." Andrew didn't relinquish his hold of the youngster, who was staring at him intently.

"How do you know so much? Aren't you just a blackamoor?"

Andrew's smile deepened. "Did you think to insult me, young lady? I am acquainted with a great many blacks and most of them have more intelligence and manners than some white people I know."

"Thank you, sir," puffed the old governess as she came trotting up to the pair. She had a delicate bone structure and an aristocratic nose and spoke in a refined, if crisp, voice.

"Elizabeth, it's time you cleaned up for nuncheon." She gave Polly a firm push in the direction of the front door. "Pardon me, sir. The child has made me forget my manners. May I be of service to you?"

It was plain to Andrew that the woman was a lady of quality fallen on hard times.

Andrew charmed the old woman with a single smile. His eyes softened and white teeth showed well against his darkly tanned skin. "I'm here to speak to Squire Satterleigh. Is he in?"

A sad look entered the faded gray eyes. "I'm sorry to say that he passed away about four weeks ago. It was an accident. Now

with the news coming today that Master Sidney is gravely
wounded in France, poor Miss Sharisse will still be left to
managing the place herself."

Andrew frowned and studied the woman closely. "You say
Lieutenant Satterleigh is in France?"

The poor governess hurried into speech to cover her dis-
comfiture at the man's apparent dissatisfaction. "Yes, Miss
Sharisse just got an official letter from India to say he'd been
sent to a hospital in Paris. The dear boy." She sniffed violently.
"We are all praying for him." The old governess took out a
well-used scrap of linen and wiped her eyes once more. "It's
almost more than a body can bear."

Andrew mulled his thoughts over for a moment. "Would it
be possible for me to speak to Miss Satterleigh? I would like to
confirm the details with her." He wondered just how Miss
Sharisse would take that news. A glance in the direction Polly
had taken told him that the girl had heard the whole, for she
had a distinctly brooding expression as she peeked about the
bush.

What a family! There was more here than met the eye, and if
Sharisse had the same lovely bone structure as Elizabeth, well,
he'd just have to pursue the end of this tale.

CHAPTER TWO

The old governess led Andrew to the front of the house. "Miss Sharisse ought to have a gentleman about to help her with the estate and things. It just isn't fitting for a lady to have to worry herself to death."

Andrew accepted the fact that the old woman was giving him license to intervene in the present circumstances.

"Isn't there a male cousin or relative to assume the duties?"

"We have never heard of one. Anyway Miss Sharisse doesn't think she needs help. But you mark my words, she's going to be shriveled up like a charred chicken wing if she doesn't slow down. What she wants is a gentleman like yourself to take matters in hand."

"Thank you for your kind words, Miss . . . ?"

"Roberts. I've been with Miss Sharisse since she was a babe. The way you handled Miss Elizabeth tells me all I need to know about yourself." She sniffed.

A young stableboy came trotting across the lawn to relieve Andrew of his horses, putting a stop to the enlightening conversation. Andrew gave the lad a quiet thanks, his eyes on the retreating figure of the governess. He was thoughtful as he strode up the flagstone walk to the massive front door of the old hall. Anyone who could inspire that kind of loyalty intrigued him. Miss Sharisse Satterleigh must be unique.

At the first knock the door was thrown open by a stoop-shouldered elderly man with only a fringe of white hair. His eyes squinted at the visitor, and he motioned him inside.

Andrew withdrew a card from his notecase and placed it on the silver salver perched on the buffet by the door. "I'd like to speak to Miss Satterleigh. I have some business with her."

The old butler didn't read the card, but the cultured voice reassured him. "Please come this way." He escorted Andrew through the main hall with a broad, curved staircase at the end to a small parlor.

Andrew had barely time to note the grand furnishings that were slowly fading with the passage of time and a detailed watercolor that could only have been done by Lawrence, when the door opened.

A tall, lissome young lady walked in, head held high, her manner one of quiet dignity as she crossed the room. Andrew noted the eyes bright with unshed tears, but it was her only concession to the ordeal he suspected she had recently been through. Andrew was appreciative of the nicely defined cleavage and the gently rounded curve of her hip as she moved toward him. He also noted the delicate bone structure that shaped her oval face.

Sharisse stared at the man, taking in his brown countenance and his long, lean figure. She noted his plain but well-cut clothes and the neat but not stylish knot to his tie. He wore no jewelry or fobs to proclaim his affluence, but Sharisse suspected that there was more to the man than met the eye. Her father had been an advocate of good boots and she'd learned more than she ever cared to know over the years. With her practiced eye, she deemed the pair in front of her to be of the finest quality. A paradox, that's what the man was.

"Miss Satterleigh? I'm Andrew Lindley. I've just come from Delhi. I had the pleasure of meeting your brother there at one of the regimental balls." He gauged her reactions to his opening salvo and decided that she would make an excellent card player.

"I'm happy to meet a friend of my brother's. I'm sorry he hasn't arrived home as yet to greet you, but you may have heard he was taken to a hospital in Paris for treatment of a head wound." She studied him carefully to see how he accepted the lie, but could discern nothing from the polite visage.

"Are you perhaps going to join him?"

Did the man suspect anything? "I don't believe that would be wise at this time. I don't think that I can help Sidney by running off to France." She could not afford to have him think she had no feeling for her brother, but she must make her position clear.

A distinct twinkle gleamed in Andrew's eye as he agreed very blandly, "I believe that you're right. You wouldn't be much help in France."

Sharisse almost gasped. It was as if he knew the whole. She dismissed the thought out of hand because she couldn't imagine his knowing and not taxing her with the tale. "I have my hands full here with the estate. Moreover, I must not leave Polly unattended." Sharisse felt the situation was moving out of her control.

"That makes much more sense," he approved. "I should have thought of that." He paused for a moment and then dropped his next lure. "Mr. Conroy, the Commissioner at Delhi had a package he asked me to deliver to your home. I believe it's some of the things Lieutenant Satterleigh . . . forgot to take with him."

That pause made Sharisse prickle with apprehension. Was he on to her scheme? She seemed to vacillate back and forth. Squaring her shoulders, she took a deep breath. "He probably wasn't conscious when they moved him. I'm sorry you were troubled." She managed to keep her voice steady. She must end this interview before she went off with apoplexy. She must be all about in the head, for not only did this man seem to have a hint of their secret, he was playing havoc with her insides. She felt alternating cold chills chasing themselves up and down her spine and distinct heat waves radiating from her middle.

"I don't mind a bit, Miss Satterleigh. If at any time I may be of service to you, please feel free to call upon me."

"I'm certain that you're a very busy man, Mr. Lindley."

"I have been over the years, but now I'm only as busy as I want to be."

They stood somewhat awkwardly for a moment and then

Sharisse found refuge in her company manners. "Would you care for some refreshment? You must have traveled a distance to get here."

"Thank you, I'd appreciate a drink." He noted the nervous movements of her hands.

Sharisse pulled the bell cord and then motioned him to a comfortable chair. The old butler appeared so promptly that she almost smiled. He had been hovering about.

"Miss Sharisse?" The old man waited for her request.

Sharisse couched her request gently and the butler replied at his most stately, "Very good, miss."

Andrew watched the interchange with interest. It was plain that the old servant regarded his mistress with the utmost respect. Sharisse Satterleigh seemed to have the complete devotion of her staff.

"Were you visiting India?" Sharisse tried to cover her unease.

"No, I was sent there in disgrace some years back. You might say I'm the black sheep of my family." When she said nothing, he continued. "I committed the folly of running off with the daughter of a prominent politician. As I look back on the experience, I'm certain that she thought I had a deal of money. When my father forcibly packed me off to India to remove me from her presence, I found that he had done me a favor. I liked the country and the climate suited me rather well. I found I had a head for business, so I can't repine for the years I lost." He smiled as he made the pronouncement, and his eyes danced with a hint of mischief.

Sharisse suspected that the man was trying to shock her but was saved from a reply, for at that moment Simms tottered into the room carrying a tray with two glasses, a bottle of wine, and one of ratafia.

Andrew jumped up and in spite of the old man's protests, took it from the bony hands and placed it on the small table by the window.

"Thank you, Simms." Sharisse gave the old man a fond smile, but her mind was considering Andrew's youthful folly.

Much could be forgiven a man who'd made his fortune, but Andrew wasn't wearing any of the noticeable signs, except for his boots. That thought alone gave her pause. She didn't hold his past indiscretion against him. It was rather hard when the man made fun of himself and, more, she liked his easy manner. But she would be a fool to cultivate his acquaintance. He rattled her more than she cared to admit and she couldn't seem to maintain the direction of a conversation with the man. He would have her confessing the whole and she and Polly would be in the suds.

As Simms turned to leave, he squinted at Andrew as if trying to get a better look. Something he saw must have reassured him, for he nodded and slowly plodded from the room.

Andrew picked up the ratafia and poured a glass for her and then a liberal portion of wine for himself. "Surely that poor soul should be retired?"

"Simms could have retired anytime these past ten years, but he's always begged me to keep him on. He's alone, his wife having died years ago, and they had no children." The words brought the fact of Sidney's death rushing back to her and her eyes showed their grief.

Andrew took a healthy swallow of his wine and teased her gently. "Now that I've confessed my worst sins, won't you tell me yours?"

She laughed and refused his gambit, but her mind darted back and forth between her problem and the story he'd just related about his youth. She couldn't help but feel that this man had suffered more than enough for his youthful sins. However, he needn't think that she was going to fall victim to his charms, great though they might be. She was in enough of a pickle without complicating the situation. "Are you planning to reside in London?"

"I do have a London town house, but as a matter of fact, I prefer to live in the country. My father has a country estate not far from here that my solicitor tells me has been willed to me, so I plan to spend a deal of time there."

"I'm acquainted with everyone for miles around and I can't think of which one it could be."

"Do you know where Brookfield Hall is?"

"Oh, you must be a relative of Edgar Wallencourt, the man who had the farm next to Brookfield Hall. It is a very nice estate, in spite of its small size. I'll wager that you're quite happy to have been informed that you are the new owner. The last I heard was that no heirs had been found."

"I am quite delighted to have a property in this part of the country because it will bring me closer to you, my pretty little darling."

Sharisse stood up, stung by the carelessness of his remark. "I'll have you know that I'm not little. In fact I'm so tall that I can look down on most men of my acquaintance. And furthermore, I'm not the slightest bit pretty. I can see quite well, thank you, and I know exactly how plain I am."

Andrew merely stood up and pulled her to him.

Sharisse gritted her teeth and ground out, "Unhand me, you . . ." Her eyes glinted sparks. "If this is a sample of Indian manners, I feel sorry for the ladies that must reside there."

"You must let me be the judge of whether or not you're pretty. I assure you I was considered quite knowledgeable in my day and I doubt that the standards have changed overly much. You may not be a diamond of the first water, but you'll stand out at any gathering. What you've got in abundance, my darling, is charm."

He tightened his arms about her for a moment and lowered his mouth slowly to kiss her forehead. "I have only the highest regard for you. And as for your size, you suit me perfectly."

"Sir, you are no gentleman." Sharisse was caught between her upbringing and her clamoring senses. A lovely flush rose to her cheeks and her eyes flashed fire.

"I never claimed to be, if I recall correctly. If you would believe me, I would declare that my intentions are honorable and beg you to accept me as a husband who would cherish you as you deserve. But if I did that you'd probably think I had sun poisoning."

Her laugh was a delight to hear. "At the very least. I am aware that you must be some type of an expert in the petticoat line, but I pray you excuse me from your endeavors, you . . . rake."

"Reformed rake, my pretty innocent," he corrected.

"I wish that I may see it," she retorted.

"You shall, but not just yet. I find that I have a bit of the rake left in me yet, for I find I can't keep myself from kissing your sweet lips."

Sharisse gasped as his mouth settled over hers. This was unheard of in one's own home. The gentleness of the kiss was unexpected and the strength of the arms stroking her back and holding her neck was almost more than she could stand. She battled her senses, trying in vain to keep her head, but her body slumped against the superior force and allowed itself to be molded against his rock-hard frame. A small cry escaped her throat as he assumed more liberties with her mouth, tasting, touching, and exploring with his marauding tongue. Finally, he set her aside reluctantly and waited for her fury to unleash itself.

She was a little slow to recover from the devastating embrace, but as she realized how complete her surrender had been, her eyes began to blaze with anger. "You . . . blackguard." With the words she doubled up her fist and swung at him viciously.

He caught it easily with one of his larger, callused hands and brought it to his lips and kissed it. "Ttt-ttt, little darling. The ladies of my acquaintance wouldn't dare to strike anyone in anger."

"You'll have to excuse me, but the provocation was more than I could bear." Her foot stamped angrily.

"I admit it. Did you know your eyes flash like a bolt of lightning when you're angry? I'd like to say that I'm sorry, but I can't find it in me to lie. I love your spirit. In fact, I love everything about you." Before she could find her tongue, he added, "Let's cry truce. I'm going to be a neighbor of yours and we really should be friends."

To Sharisse, the words were a dash of cold water. How did one fight the strong emotions that Andrew called up within her when he changed the front of attack before she could draw the battle lines? "If you promise to behave yourself, I think that I could try. But I do believe that being in India you've lost touch with the civilized world."

He gave a crack of laughter. He'd never seen greater sticklers for propriety than he'd met in India. And when the occasion demanded it, he fit the mold quite well. But had never before had the desire to conform to the role full time. "I'll be your most devoted pupil. What shall we talk about first? Politics? How about horses? I saw a magnificent hunter being led about in the stableyard as I drove up. Does he belong to you?"

"We have an entire stable of hunters. I can't think which one you might mean."

"This was a black with a blaze on his forehead and looked to be very spirited. The reason I ask is because I find that I would like to buy him if you could be convinced to sell him."

"Black Devil was my father's hunter. No one else can ride him. He's a great jumper and has remarkable speed, but has a nasty habit of trying to bite anyone who comes near him." The stableboys were frightened to death of the animal. What had he seen? If by some chance Black Devil were what Andrew was looking for, it just might solve her immediate financial problems. She couldn't use the rent moneys, because they were earmarked for preservation of the estate.

Andrew laughed, his eyes soft with something that Sharisse couldn't quite put a name to.

"That's no way to sell a horse. Let's try this again. You tell me all his good points and I'll try to find out his less desirable ones."

Sharisse smiled at his banter. "My father was often the first on the scene at the kill at a hunt when he rode Black Devil. And father always said that the horse was intrepid."

"That's better," he approved. "Would you have time to show me this paragon of horseflesh? I think that we might come to terms."

Sharisse was certain that he was only funning her, but she couldn't afford to miss the opportunity if it presented itself. She shook out her skirts and led the way through the french doors.

They walked leisurely toward the stables, Sharisse with a deal of determination showing in the tilt of her chin, and Andrew with an enigmatic smile as he followed behind her. He was very much taken with the fetching picture she made, her gown showing a hint of the willowy figure concealed beneath and her copper curls bouncing.

One of the stableboys ran out to meet them. The lad strode with a coltish gait that showed his immaturity, but he aimed to please with every gesture. It was plain that the young man was trying to prove his worth.

"Clem, will you please saddle Black Devil?" She gave the youngster a warm smile and he scurried off to do her bidding, his face wreathed in an answering smile.

They stood idly talking for a few moments and then were interrupted by a crusty voice bellowing, "Na then, ye black beggar, stand!" This was followed by several thumps that Andrew interpreted to be the stallion kicking the sides of the enclosure, and a string of imprecations from the head groom.

Andrew looked at Sharisse, but she didn't appear to be overly concerned, so he held his peace. In another moment a huge black stallion appeared, held on either side by Cowley, the head groom, and Clem. The horse was snorting, tossing his head about, and lashing out with his heels, protesting every foot of the way.

Andrew watched the magnificent beast and catalogued his virtues. The horse was over fifteen and a half hands high, his eyes were large, clear, and wide set, and he had a silky black coat. Andrew gauged the horse to be strong in the withers, have powerful legs, and overall to be a treasure at any price.

Sharisse noted how taken Andrew seemed to be with the animal. Now it remained to be seen if he were capable of riding him. A shiver of anticipation ran through her as she watched Andrew approach the plunging horse. She wouldn't want him to be injured, but it might be amusing to see him get his comeuppance.

Andrew was speaking to the animal in low tones and the beast seemed to calm down a bit. He stroked the strong neck and quietly took the reins from Clem while motioning the men away. In one swift motion he was firmly in the saddle. The horse sidestepped a bit and tossed his head, but seemed to know that this was a force to be reckoned with.

Cowley stood scratching his almost bald head, his face a mixture of puzzlement and respect.

Andrew gently put his heels to the horse and set him on the path to the tenant farms.

Sharisse noted his mastery of the spirited creature that she previously had thought to be uncontrollable. Andrew Lindley was nothing that she had expected and certainly not the gentleman of her dreams, but she couldn't deny the strength of her attraction to him.

As she stood looking after his retreating figure with a rueful grin, Polly stalked up to her. "What's that man doing riding Black Devil?" She scowled fiercely.

"He knew Sidney in India and stopped to bring me his belongings."

Polly's childish mouth formed a silent "O." "Does he know about Sidney?"

"He didn't seem to. He said these were things Sidney had left behind. Surely if he knew Sidney was dead he'd have confronted me with the fact."

"The sooner we get rid of him the better," Polly muttered to herself, fully aware that Sharisse wasn't listening. Polly had a few ideas of how she could discourage the man if he seemed persistent. The mischief was so bright in her eyes that it danced. If Sharisse had been looking at Polly instead of down the lane, she would have known that Polly was up to no good, but her mind was still with the skillful rider. Those hands seemed to possess a lean strength, but they also showed a careful gentleness.

CHAPTER THREE

Polly folded her arms and pursed her lips while she waited for Sharisse's attention. "Well?"

As Andrew disappeared completely from view, Sharisse turned to her younger sister and smiled. "Did you want to say something, darling?"

"He's awfully brown, isn't he?" Polly waited for Sharisse's reaction.

"I believe that comes from his being in India for so long. The color will fade with time." She didn't add that it didn't detract in the slightest from his aura of virility. She chastised herself as the thought jumped into her mind. She didn't quite know what to do with thoughts such as that. Never before had she felt this way.

Polly tried again. "He doesn't look as if he has a feather to fly with."

"Polly!" Sharisse almost shrieked her horror.

"Well, I don't see a thing to recommend him," Polly sniffed.

Sharisse failed to note the injured tone. "I don't believe that you noted his boots. Father always said you could judge a man by his boots, and Mr. Lindley's are in the style of Hoby's."

"Are you defending him, Sharisse?" the little girl whispered. Polly's eyes had grown quite large and she was more than worried that her sister might form an attachment for Mr. Lindley. Polly had decided that the man wouldn't do. She didn't like his high-handed manner or his plain speaking, which put her in the wrong. She was used to having her every wish granted and so she determined to throw a bit of rock in the way of his wheels, so to speak.

Sharisse gave Polly a searching look. "Do you know something that I don't? Out with it, young lady!"

Polly was busily thinking up the most outrageous tales. "Well, I . . . ."

Andrew happened to choose that moment to canter back into the stableyard and Polly was spared answering.

He swung down easily and handed the reins to Cowley, who had come running out of the stable. The old groom led the horse away to cool him out.

"Hello, Elizabeth. Have you settled your differences with your governess?" He raised one eyebrow at the girl in amusement, but Polly merely scowled at him.

Sharisse ignored her sister's manners. "How did you meet Polly?" She hoped that the youngster hadn't given away any information.

"We more or less ran into each other in the carriageway." Andrew's eyes twinkled as he winked at Polly, but Sharisse missed the exchange, as she was busy assessing the little girl, who still scowled.

Polly glared, waiting for Andrew to tell her sister about her bad manners, but he said nothing more about the subject. When Polly realized that the conversation had turned to more grown-up subjects, she snorted and stalked back to the house. The man was obviously going to wait to tell Sharisse until she was out of the way. Polly figured that it was bad enough to tattle about her when she was there to defend herself, but inexcusable to tattle about someone when she couldn't fight back. Before she was out of earshot, she overheard Sharisse inviting the fellow to stay for nuncheon. With an evil grin, Polly began to run.

"I wonder what's gotten into Polly. She's usually such a well-mannered child." She apologized perfunctorily as she contemplated what Polly had been about to say. She donned her best smile and tossed her head to one side. "Perhaps I should ask if you are interested in Black Devil?"

The warmth of the smile that returned hers caused Sharisse's stomach to contract with a peculiar feeling that amazed her. The man couldn't be called handsome even by the most generous of standards, but nonetheless, she was attracted to him. He was almost overwhelming. He carried an air of command, yet he seemed gentle. He was blatantly masculine, yet she didn't wish to be aware of the fact. The few men who had previously set out to dazzle her had been more charming and more polished. It made her puzzle even harder what it was about the man that intrigued her.

"If you're certain that you'd like to sell him, I'm prepared to make you an offer."

Sharisse gave him a saucy grin. "My papa always said never to talk business on an empty stomach and I have always followed his advice. Why don't we have our nuncheon first and then discuss the horse?"

"I applaud your strategy. A man is always more mellow after he's been fed." His teasing was light and his eyes softened as he watched her.

"In that case, I hope cook has outdone herself." Sharisse found she was enjoying the light repartee immensely.

"You may be wise. I find that my appetite is very large." He gave her an appreciative leer.

Sharisse tried to look offended, but his little-boy antics were ridiculous and she succumbed to a trill of laughter.

"I love to hear you laugh. It improves your appearance dramatically. I shall see to it that I entertain you often."

"Am I so ugly that I must needs smile all the time?"

"Did I imply that you are less than desirable?" He shook his head despairingly. "My talent for turning a pretty phrase has deserted me. I am undone. What am I to do?" He paused with a ridiculous expression on his face to see how his dramatics were being received.

The plea was so forlorn that Sharisse laughed yet again. "Sir, I protest. I can not laugh anymore. My side hurts from your drollery."

"Then I shall have to be serious for a moment. Has no man ever extolled your virtues? I assure you they are many."

She simply nodded.

"I thought I could not be the first to say that your eyes are like the stars. A man could spend a lifetime looking into them to see all their wonders."

As they entered the house, Sharisse beamed her pleasure at his company and motioned him to the stairs at the end of the hall. "If you'd like to use our guest room to wash up, you're welcome. Take the first door on your left at the top of the stairs. We have nuncheon in the breakfast room, since Polly and I are usually alone. It's just down the hall."

He nodded and proceeded up the curved staircase with a jaunty step. Sharisse watched out of the corner of her eye as she turned for the kitchen. She found that the man had a decisiveness about him that reminded her of her father and she wondered if she dared chance allowing him to set up a flirtation. No! she told herself rationally.

Her experience with men had taught her that she wasn't in the usual way. This man seemed to be a far cry from the usual town dandy and she found she liked the difference immensely, but she was still wary.

Now—with the situation being such—mayhap she'd have to take Polly's childish suggestion seriously and determine if it was possible to find a husband who could provide for both of them and allow her to house Polly in a manner to which she was accustomed. Andrew Lindley seemed to be just what Polly had ordered, even if the child didn't realize it yet.

She resolved to get to the family solicitor and find out just how critical the need was to pursue such a course. If Sidney had by some chance provided for her and Polly in a will, then possibly things might not be so desperate as she thought.

If there were money, she could take her time to look about at all the current beaux on the marriage mart. She grew excited as she thought about another London season, for now she was old enough to know her mind and not take offense at the callow youths who once had spurned her.

She walked on to the butler's pantry and called, "Simms?"

The old man rose from his work polishing the silver and bowed respectfully. "Yes, miss?"

"Would you inform cook that we will have a guest for nuncheon?"

"Very good, miss," replied the old man promptly, but his white brows rose at the unusual event.

Sharisse rearranged some flowers from one of the vases on the buffet in the hall and brought them to the breakfast-room table. She surveyed the room with detached approval. The sideboard held a large silver tea tray and some fragile pieces of old Ming porcelain. The room had an attractive air, with its décor in tones of amber and rust.

Seeing that everything was in perfect order, including the extra place setting, she gave an audible sigh of relief. It would have been more proper to serve Andrew in the small dining room, but she preferred the warmth and brightness of the breakfast room.

Polly slid into the room with what Sharisse called the youngster's angelic look. The child was up to mischief and Sharisse tried to imagine what Polly could have done this time.

The real clue was that Polly sat quietly waiting for their guest with a nonchalant air, like the well-bred child she was purported to be. Her hair had been rebraided and her face washed and Polly hadn't even complained about the clean pinafore that her governess had insisted upon. That in itself was most unusual and coupled with the fact that her glance kept darting from Sharisse to the door, it confirmed Sharisse's suspicion that someone was going to be the victim of one of Polly's pranks. Which one of the servants would it be this time, she mused idly.

Andrew opened the door to the green bedchamber and walked to the bowl and pitcher set on the commode. He picked up the pitcher and poured a generous amount of water in the flowered china bowl. As he did so he spied a small turtle floating in it, swimming vigorously.

He stared incredulously at the small creature. How on earth could it have gotten into the pitcher? As he picked up the small reptile and examined it closely, he discerned a scratched "P" on its shell. He began to chuckle. "Well, Miss Polly Satterleigh, I see that you're trying to give me a message, but I don't believe that I'm going to take your advice. Instead, I'm going to teach you a lesson that someone should have given you long ago." Polly was backing the wrong horse if she thought that he was that flighty. There was nothing he liked better than a challenge, and that little lady had just thrown down the gauntlet. He put the turtle carefully in his pocket and cleansed his hands in the questionable water. He was still smiling as he dried his hands on the spotless linen and he whistled as he tripped lightly down the stairs. He'd find a way to return the child's pet without her sister's knowledge. He'd never been one to spoil someone's lark.

He found the breakfast room without trouble and Sharisse waved him to a seat. Polly's eyes were glued on him. As he took his seat he flashed Polly such a warm smile that Sharisse was amazed. What had Polly been up to that she deserved such a grin? She rang for Simms, pondering if Andrew could have been the victim of one of Polly's jokes, but from the look on his face she dismissed the thought out of hand.

When Sharisse took the time to notice Polly, she found that her young sister's nose was a titch out of joint. What on earth could have gotten into the child? She was glaring at Andrew and he was grinning from ear to ear.

The repast was simple but it was apparent that Andrew enjoyed both the meal and the company. He kept the conversation moving with a series of humorous stories about some of his adventures in Delhi and made several lighthearted jokes at his own expense. Sharisse was enthralled and even Polly couldn't keep her eyes away from him.

As the meal came to a close Andrew suddenly stood, moved the few steps to Polly's chair, and reached to the floor. "I believe you lost something." He palmed the small turtle into the pocket of her pinafore and then returned to his seat.

Polly looked clearly shocked, wide eyes staring at him.

"What did you drop, Polly?" Sharisse demanded.

The child was unable to answer and Andrew broke in smoothly. "I believe it's a shell. Perhaps a favorite toy?"

"Thank you," was all that Polly could choke out.

Sharisse frowned at her sister. "How many times have I told you not to bring things to the table?"

"Don't be too hard on her. I can remember when I was her age I did a lot worse."

Polly's shoulders sagged in temporary relief, but she flashed him an angry glare. "May I be excused?" She liked him even less, since he couldn't be man enough to speak up in her presence. Would he try to speak to her alone?

Sharisse nodded absently. She was anxious to get on with the negotiations with Andrew. She'd been trying to figure out a price, but couldn't quite bring herself to ask the ridiculous figure that her father had paid for the creature.

Sharisse conducted Andrew to the back drawing room. When they were ensconced in the set of wing chairs by the window, she asked easily, "Shall we begin?"

"Are you certain that your brother won't want this horse for himself? I understand he's an unusually good horseman."

Sharisse turned her head abruptly to look out the window and swallowed convulsively. She must get herself under control. Andrew didn't have the slightest suspicion of her deceit. If Sidney were alive, it was true, there would be no need to sell the horse, but then Sidney had never been enamored of the animal, so Sharisse didn't have any compunctions about saying so. Since Andrew seemed to want her to conduct this sale like a proper business deal, she'd use the techniques that she'd heard her father use from the ancient way of the Chinese.

"Sidney never liked Black Devil. I believe that he'd be happy to see him go to someone who would get some use from him."

"That sounds decisive. You're certain that you want to sell him?"

"Yes. I would like to see you have him." And she would be more than grateful of the money that the sale would bring.

"What are you asking for him?" Andrew's eyes mesmerized Sharisse as she stared intently at him.

She shook her head a bit as if to clear her mind and then

began with a rush. "I know my father paid over a thousand pounds for him. But I think that I . . ." She held her breath for fear he couldn't meet the price she had decided upon when he interrupted her.

"Now, that's not the way to sell a horse. Let me help you. You start by saying the horse is worth every bit of fifteen hundred pounds.

"Fifteen hundred," she parroted dutifully, wondering what he knew about Chinese bartering. Her father had introduced her to all the nuances but she never before had tried it.

"I answer that fifteen hundred is a bit more than I think he's worth. I'll offer a thousand pounds."

"A thousand! You are all about in your head!" Sharisse was appalled at how easily this had become a game.

"Now you're catching on! So you won't consider a thousand?" How about eleven hundred?"

"Eleven hundred?" she murmured skeptically, noting the banter in his voice. "I don't believe that you understand how much has gone into training the animal."

"Not enough? Very well, would you consider eleven fifty?"

"I don't believe that I could accept that." She grinned, knowing he was deliberately pushing up the price.

"Twelve hundred pounds is my last offer. How about it?"

He looked so innocent that she laughed. The man was an actor past price. From what she could discern of his expression, he was utterly serious, but the crinkling about his eyes bespoke his laughter.

"Have you no proper feelings, laughing at a man's best offer?" His words were heavy, but the mocking tone affirmed his humor. "I'm not prepared to spend more," he assured her, with an almost straight face.

"What do you know about the horse that I don't? I believe that I must reconsider selling him. Black Devil will make a magnificent stud for our stable."

"I believe that his temperament precludes such a thought. The horse is clearly a menace to the stable hands and possibly to you and Polly. What if Polly should take it into her head that she can ride the beast?"

Sharisse shook her head as if considering changing her mind about the sale. "Still, Black Devil has good bloodlines and I think that Polly will stay away from him. If you will consider thirteen hundred, I believe that I can be persuaded to part with him."

Andrew was enjoying himself thoroughly. The minx knew that he was interested and was going to make him part with every penny that she thought she could get away with. She was in every way suited for him. He couldn't have bargained any better himself. It spoke volumes for his self-control to be able to reply with a seeming indifference, "I might go as high as twelve hundred and fifty, but that is my last offer."

"I think that I can force myself to accept that paltry sum, but you realize that you're stealing Black Devil at that price. All the training that has been spent on Black Devil since we acquired him makes him quite a prize." She concluded the bargain in the accepted oriental manner.

Andrew agreed quickly and stretched out his hand to hers. "Shake on it?"

Sharisse accepted the strong, warm hand in bemused silence. Was that all there was to it? Had she been swindled or had she gotten the best deal? At this point she didn't know.

"I do have one favor to ask." Andrew's eyes twinkled his pleasure as he watched the confusion on her face.

"Yes?" she asked, slightly breathlessly. Was there to be a condition attached?

"I haven't had a chance to inspect my stables and they may not be fit to house Black Devil. May I leave him here for a few days?" It was a plausible excuse for coming to visit every day.

"Certainly. I have no objection. It will give you time to change your mind about our agreement."

"Sharisse, I'm disappointed in you," he scolded gently.

"I beg your pardon?" she asked uneasily.

"Your lack of faith in me. I see that I have a large job ahead of me teaching you to trust me. When I make a decision, I don't change my mind. I'm one of the steadfast things of this world, darling. Remember that." He picked up the hand he had shaken seconds before and raised it gallantly to his lips.

Lights danced behind her eyes and sparks ignited. Shivers chased themselves around her back and she felt that her legs wouldn't hold her much longer. He sensed the softening in her demeanor and swept her into his arms.

Gently he kissed her lips and Sharisse forgot the rest of the world. Suddenly she was a dove soaring in the sky, drifting through the clouds, and glorying in the warmth of the sun. Far too soon the sensations receded and she was aware of what had happened. Her face showed shock and embarrassment.

"Don't worry, my darling. I'll be gentle with you. I'll never take more than you're willing to offer me." He put his finger to her lips to silence her when she would have spoken. "You are a lady beyond price and I value you highly." With the words, he was gone.

Sharisse didn't quite know what to make of the man. One minute he had her laughing and the next she was almost swooning at his feet. She couldn't decide which was sillier, letting herself be swept off her feet by this foreign-looking Lothario or not letting herself explore the feelings that he aroused.

It was a very dreamy Sharisse who went on about her chores that afternoon. Was she believing a fairy tale or could there be such a one as Prince Charming? The possibilities seemed endless, and for the first time since she had read about Sidney's death she felt a glimmer of hope.

CHAPTER FOUR

Andrew tooled his horses briskly over the dirt track to Brook-field Hall. His smile was deep and he chuckled to himself. Life seemed to have taken an interesting turn and he was already looking forward to the next confrontation with the engaging young lady.

He had been bothered by her deception at first, knowing that the Commissioner's letter would have told of Sidney's demise. After all, he had been in the office when the news arrived via an agent dressed as a native. The entire patrol had been wiped out. Bodies were strewn over the forest, so muti-lated that it was almost impossible to discern the identities of the men. A detail had retrieved the bodies but two were unaccounted for. It was thought that tigers had dragged them off.

Andrew had been glad to sell out his holdings and return home. In spite of the good Lord Mornington had accom-plished years before with the Indian unrest, there were still sporadic outbursts of hostilities.

His mind returned to Sharisse and the puzzle she presented. He was fairly certain that the reason for her deception lay in the fact that the estate was entailed and that the property would fall from her hands when Sidney's death was an-nounced. He surmised that Sharisse and Polly hadn't been provided for in either will and that his dear delight was look-ing about her to see what alternatives were open to her.

His lips quirked upward. She didn't need to worry. He was going to take care of both of them—whether she willed it or not. He was not a man to brook much opposition, but in this instance he would first try to accomplish his objectives with the ways of a gentleman. His biggest hurdle seemed to be how to keep her from being ostracized by the *ton* for marrying him. His aunts could help him if they would. He wondered how they would receive him after all these years.

As he mulled the problem over, he swung the curricle into the carriage drive of Brookfield Hall, noting that the lawns were wild with neglect. His eye swept over the entire scene before him and he could almost hear the buildings screaming their neglect. His jaw hardened as he saw the miserable state of disrepair. He'd heard that his father had become a recluse in the past few years, but he'd had no idea of the extent of his failure of stewardship.

He drove around to the stables, with little hope that a stable-boy would be available. He put the horses into two of the old stalls and found them some grain and water. He noticed an old cob standing in one stall and patted the animal. "I guess I have you to thank for there being some kind of fodder for my cattle."

He sighed his dissatisfaction as he strode up to the front door and banged the knocker sharply. He waited impatiently for a few moments before it was opened by a man in his shirt sleeves. Andrew guessed him to be about fifty and could tell by his dress that times were hard.

"Yes, sir?" The butler scrutinized this stranger, while waiting to hear what he had to say. It was plain that the servant didn't find anything extraordinary in Andrew's dress.

Andrew merely raised an eyebrow in amusement and he let the man look his fill. He finally reached for his note case and extended a card. "I am Andrew Lindley, Lord Brookfield, and have come to look over my estate."

"Your pardon, Your Lordship," the man gulped in surprise. "I had no idea . . ." The man stammered his excuses as he stepped back and threw the door open wide. He rubbed the back of his neck in a gesture of inadequacy.

Andrew stepped in and took in the desolate hall. All the furniture was under Holland covers and the paintings had been removed from the walls. Andrew took off his hat and gloves and tossed them on a small table. "How long has Brookfield Hall been in this condition?"

The steely tone made the man flinch. "Mrs. Adams and I have been alone these past two years. I've been butler here for the last ten and my wife acts as housekeeper. Old Lord Brookfield closed this place down and we were kept on as caretakers. He didn't see fit to give us the money to hire anyone to help." The man's eyes pleaded for understanding. "The old hall here deserves more, but we each have only two hands."

Andrew listened but made no comment. He turned and opened a door on his left that led to the study. "Fetch Mrs. Adams to me. I need to talk to you both."

Adams's face turned gray and he gulped despairingly as he hurried down the hall to find his wife. He mumbled, "Lord have mercy, we've done the best we could."

When the couple returned, Andrew was ensconced in a large Chippendale chair and was sitting comfortably with his long legs stretched out before him. He looked the couple over critically, liking the honesty he saw and the protective air Adams had toward his frightened spouse.

"I want to restore the Hall to its rightful glory. It will be a great undertaking and I will expect much hard work. I suspect it will take a mountain of servants. Do you think that you both can handle overseeing such a project?"

Adams smiled for the first time. "Yes, Your Lordship. We can do it. The missus and I are capable. In the old days we handled a large staff and would very much like the opportunity to serve again. You won't be sorry."

Mrs. Adams nodded her approval of her husband's words.

"Good. I am a hard taskmaster, but I pay exceedingly well. Anyone who doesn't meet my standards will find that I'll make short shrift of him. Those who stay with me can count on a decent pension when the time comes."

Mrs. Adams began to fidget about and wring her hands.

"Well?" Andrew didn't take well to those who beat about the bush.

"If you please, Your Lordship, will there be enough money to replace some of the linens and restock the larder?"

Andrew's look softened. "There is all the money you'll need, but I don't tolerate waste or misuse. I expect a full accounting for every penny spent at the end of each month." He explained what he expected and what types of expenses they could incur without consulting him. They nodded in agreement.

A look of understanding passed between the couple that spoke volumes for the respect that they had for this man's grasp of financial details. They knew that they could use every shilling they needed and not a penny more.

Andrew gave Adams a list of instructions and told him to see to the preliminary work of sorting out applicants for the positions that were available. "I'll trust your judgment to a point, but I will give final approval. Don't worry about a cook. I'll see to that when I'm in London next."

When the arrangements were concluded, Andrew smiled generously. He had found long ago that a kind word and a smile went a good distance to getting people to help him. "Now I suggest you make the master bedchamber fit for me and find me something edible for my dinner."

The Adamses returned the grin and turned hastily toward the kitchen to do his bidding.

"I believe that the Lord has smiled on us for a change, Mary." Adams prepared to go to the henhouse and kill a chicken.

His wife started clanging pans, opening different bins, and pouring varying amounts into a bowl, stirring as she moved. "If this is smiling, I sure don't want him to grin."

Sharisse drew an audible sigh of relief as she heard the door close behind Andrew. The man was potent. He was like a strong perfume, surrounding her with its essence. He seemed to be everywhere she looked. She tried valiantly to dismiss him from her thoughts.

She turned to Polly. "I know you've been into mischief. You

can't hide it from me, young lady. What was that business at the table all about? Dropping a shell?

Polly dropped her eyes and twisted her hands, wriggling in her seat. That tone invariably meant she was in the suds. Reluctantly she reached into her pocket and pulled out her little pet, extending it to her sister.

"Your turtle! Polly, you know you're not supposed to bring him to the table. It's a wonder Mr. Lindley wasn't disgusted."

Polly drew a deep breath and let it out silently, while nodding her head.

"Mr. Lindley has offered to buy Black Devil at a tremendous price. It will help tide us through the rough spots."

Polly digested this with pursed lips. "But you don't really like him, do you?" Polly's eyes were open wide and fastened on her sister.

Sharisse knew exactly what Polly meant, but chose to prevaricate. "Why, don't *you* like him?"

"Well," Polly admitted grudgingly, "he's not a slow top or a dandy, but he doesn't seem to have enough money to keep us. He doesn't dress as if he has money and all the properties about Brookfield Hall including the Hall itself have been neglected for a long time. Papa said that it was because the money had run out."

That gave Sharisse pause for thought. It would take a tidy bundle to restore any of the properties about Brookfield Hall to what they had been when Sharisse was a girl. However, Andrew's virile presence would make any home palatable. Sharisse was shocked at her unladylike thoughts.

"Never mind. Since the question of marrying Andrew hasn't arisen, I don't think we need be overly concerned over his lack of money." She wondered what she could say if the question did arise.

Polly wasn't convinced of her sister's disinterest. She looked askance at her sister, gauging the faraway look in her eyes and began plotting in earnest. "When are we going up to London so you can look for someone really special?"

Sharisse smiled tenderly at her little sister, knowing the

child had her welfare at heart. "I have a few things to do here before we go. I have to go over the books and make certain they're in order. Then I must check on the tenants and notify the bailiff."

"Will we be able to see Punch and Judy shows?"

"Of course, there will be lots of treats for you, but Miss Roberts will be along to see that you keep up with your lessons."

That drew a long face, but it didn't last. The dizzy prospect of London danced before her eyes.

Sharisse tugged gently on a red braid and Polly sighed. That was a sure sign that she was back in Sharisse's good graces. Polly gave her sister a big hug and headed for the door.

As the youngster skipped off, Sharisse turned her mind back to Andrew. She didn't find the craggy face ill-favored; if anything, it held a strange appeal. Everything about the man was different from any other man of her acquaintance. That must be the reason she was so attracted, she decided.

She'd make a trip to London soon to the family solicitor to see just how she was fixed now that Sidney was gone. It probably wouldn't be too long until her tale reached him. Sharisse wasn't one to dally once her mind was made up, and she made her way to the study.

A lot depended on what she found when she spoke to Mr. Critchfield. The man was as sharp as he could stare and she'd have to have her head screwed on tight to be able to gain information from him instead of his extracting it from her. She knew she should tell as much of the truth as possible. The trick was to decide how much was enough to get the answers she wanted without betraying herself.

She sat down at the desk; the pile of account ledgers was waiting for her. There was a determination in her chin and her head was held high. She'd make this work. After all, she was no poor simpering miss without a brain.

She lifted her quill and set herself to the task. There was at least two days' work to record and add the figures. After completing one set of entries, she sat back and stretched. The estate was doing quite well since she had taken over. The bailiff was content to have her overseeing the books. He even admitted that she had a head for business.

Sharisse lifted her quill again and began to add the rents. She shook her head as she added the column of figures for the third time. Evidently her mind was straying from the page in front of her. As she looked up an image of Andrew came to mind.

"I don't have time for you. Go away." The image seemed to laugh at her. "I'm not interested in you. I must have a man of substance, one that will be able to keep us comfortable. Polly deserves at least that." Sharisse was appalled as she realized that she was talking to herself. The man had made her daft. What was there about him that made her want to get lost in those deep green pools of his eyes?

Was it her concern for Polly that made her look closely at Andrew? Was it Andrew's property that turned her head? No, she admitted crossly.

She was drawn to him inexplicably. The man had an air of possessiveness, but it wasn't that. He had a gleam of appreciation of her womanly attributes, but it wasn't that. She'd experienced that before and not one of the men turned her head. What Andrew possessed was a dab of charm, a touch of humor, a dash of common sense, and a great deal of perception.

CHAPTER FIVE

Andrew woke early, eager to see the stables were made ready for his new hunter. When he could get to London, he would hire a head groom. He would like to have his father's groom in London if the man were still about, for he had had a fondness for Andrew when Andrew had been a lad.

As he went to the stables, a pair of sparkling brown eyes seemed to dance before him. Sharisse's face had been a delight to behold as he had transacted the sale. The darling had gotten into the spirit of the thing as she saw his intention. It was just one of the things that attracted him.

As he reached the old stone building a freckle-faced lad with light brown hair appeared in the doorway.

I'm Tim, Yer Lordship. I've curried both yer 'orses. "Ee but they're a pair of bang-up bloods, if I ever did see um!"

Andrew's eyebrows rose a full inch. Adams had indeed proved his worth in producing a much needed stableboy at the drop of a hat. "Thank you, Tim. Do you think you can pole them up for me?"

Tim's face was wreathed in smiles. "Yes, sir, Yer Lordship. I've been around 'orses since I was knee high to a beagle. M' father's head groom at Thorn Hill. Lord Winchley, what owns it, said I was too small to work for him yet, but Mr. Adams knows my pa and he said I should come to ye. I'd sure like to stay." The hopeful face looked up at Andrew.

"You put my horses to properly and you've got a job." Andrew liked to see a youngster eager to work and if he showed any ability, he'd keep the boy on. He stood for a minute or two slapping his gloves in his hand as his mind went back to Sharisse. The best way to help her would be to marry her out of hand, but that might take some doing. That young woman had a mind of her own and he didn't think she'd take kindly to the idea of marrying without the attendant folderol.

The possibilities amused him and he laughed. If any of his old cronies could hear him, they'd think he was a candidate for Bedlam. He had been laid low by a pair of sad, determined brown eyes and they had him jumping over himself to help her. It was hard to relate the mature, womanly creature that he'd confronted at the Meadows to the little girl Sidney had kept bringing into their conversations. Sidney had spoken of his sister often and they had laughed together over some of the antics the pair of them had been involved in. Andrew had grown fond of a little girl who tried to keep up with her older brother, but Sharisse was a far cry from the "little sister" he had pictured. She was all the woman any man could ask for and he meant her to be his. He laughed again. His advice to others on the fairer sex was going to come back to haunt him.

Tim appeared leading his horses, and Andrew walked about the curricle to inspect the harnesses. "You've done an excellent job. Consider yourself in my employ. I'll be hiring some other stable hands, but you are to take your orders from me and from the head groom when I hire him. Is that understood?" He bent a sharp eye to the lad.

A grin split the boy's face from ear to ear. "Yes, sir, Yer Lordship. Thank 'ee." He choked the last words out.

"You haven't asked your wages and your accommodations. What kind of a businessman are you?" Andrew asked humorously.

"Iffen ye please, if I can 'ave me food and a place to sleep . . ." Tim's voice trailed off as he looked up at his benefactor's frown.

"Nonsense. I'm sure you'll find a room of your own above the stables and you shall have five pounds a year to start."

The boy was trying very hard not to cry at the extremely generous offer, but he sniffled loudly. "A room of me own and five puns?"

Andrew nodded and clapped Tim on the shoulder. "See

what you can do about mucking out a stall for a very spirited horse I'll be bringing home within a few days."

Andrew gathered up the reins and stepped up into the curricle. With a light touch he set the horses trotting toward the Meadows. He whistled as he set the team to a spanking pace. The day was sunny and clear and fortune was smiling upon him. He had set about putting his house to order and now he would begin his campaign to win his bride.

Sharisse was poring over the estate ledger again with her quill in hand. It seemed that she had spent every spare minute in the last two days in the book room doing calculations. She jotted down figures, crossing and recrossing her lines. Her chin had a splotch of ink on it and tendrils of her auburn hair were flying loose over her cheeks. A deep frown marred her forehead as she tried unsuccessfully to balance the accounts.

She looked up in surprise as Simms announced Lord Brookfield. For just a moment she thought she was going to see the surly old recluse from Brookfield Hall, but when she beheld the fine figure of masculinity before her, she knew that Andrew had been laughing at her expense the previous day.

Andrew stood there smiling, a hint of mischief dancing in his eyes. "Good morning, my darling."

"Don't you try to flummery me, Lord Brookfield. And, pray tell, why didn't you enlighten my ignorance yesterday? It must have been quite a lark for you to see me make such a cake of myself. Forgive my forwardness, but you had no right!" She seethed in her humiliation.

Andrew admired the fetching picture she made in silence. Her eyes flashed their fire and his loins tightened as he thought of harnessing that power for his own. Her lips pursed as she finished her tirade and he moved to stand before her. Andrew pulled a square of fine linen from his pocket and dabbed the splotch of ink from her cheek.

Sharisse's bosom heaved with indignation and she readied herself to speak again.

A muscle in Andrew's cheek twitched in amusement as he

bent forward to capture her lips and silence her protests. He gently explored the soft moist recesses of her mouth and claimed them in an extremely potent act of possession.

Sharisse reeled under the onslaught and her legs grew weak as the invasion grew with intensity. Never had she felt so helpless, so caught. It was like being in the middle of a raging storm and have it breaking all about her. It was like sailing the Channel on a choppy sea. No, it was more intense than both of those. She finally gave up her introspection and let herself be drawn into the raging fire.

When Andrew finally pushed her slowly away from him, and took stock of her flushed face, slightly bruised lips, and tousled hair, he smiled his satisfaction. "You must forgive my forwardness, darling, but you tempt me sorely."

A mass of emotions flitted across her face as she realized the extent of her surrender and the impropriety of the exchange. She stamped her foot in vexation. "You lack the qualities of a gentleman, sir."

Andrew was unperturbed. "But I thought that we had already established that fact yesterday, my darling."

"I am not your darling," she gritted through clenched teeth.

"Why, certainly you are. You just don't know it yet. I assured you yesterday that my intentions are honorable." His face bespoke innocence, but a hint of a laugh lurked behind his eyes.

Sharisse studied him skeptically and finally decided to laugh at the incident. "Lord Brookfield, you are incorrigible! I must be careful not to give you even part of an inch.

"You are so wrong, my sweet one. I intend for you to give me everything."

"Enough! You are far too glib and I don't understand today's manner of funning."

Andrew shrugged his shoulders and changed his front of attack. "It seems that you have a problem," he said gently, gesturing toward the ledger. "How may I help?" He moved over to the desk, noting the neat rows of figures. "I assure you I don't have a long nose, but if it's a matter of totaling a column of figures you should know that I'm an expert. I've had years of practice."

Sharisse's smile appeared instantly. Andrew had been some sort of file clerk in India and now he'd come home to assume his rightful heritage, although there wasn't much left of it. The old Lord Brookfield had been rumored to have gambled away huge sums, and toward the end he'd shut up everything and become a recluse. It didn't portend well for the new Lord Brookfield, and Sharisse wondered just how he planned to make ends meet. The thought of his having such a struggle all his life and then coming home to another battle softened her heart. She moved to stand beside him and pointed down to one of the columns.

"I usually can tally the columns without trouble, but today they just won't cooperate." A dimple peeked out at the side of her cheek.

Andrew couldn't help but notice it and his ardor was aroused. He wanted to take her in his arms again and prove just how much she was attracted to him, but discretion won and he shook his head and grinned. "I understand perfectly. At the end of a long day, the numbers seem to dance about the page, that's when I know it's time to quit."

He pulled up a chair beside the one she'd been using and carefully blotted the ink from the paper. He reached for the quill, wiping it meticulously before dipping it in the well. Within a few minutes he crossed off one figure and added the totals. He looked up and smiled warmly. "It wasn't hard for an old expert to spot. You entered one of the rent rolls twice. I think you'll find it straight now." He turned the chair to face her. "I couldn't help but see that you're doing an excellent job of running the estates. You could hire out as an overseer."

"I enjoy it, but it wouldn't be seemly. Moreover, no one would hire me." Sharisse was drawn into the depths of his eyes.

"I would. If you are ever in need I assure you I have a place for you," he spoke seriously.

Sharisse gauged Andrew's words and decided that the man

was flirting with her. Somehow the thought was quite exhilarating. If Andrew were actually interested, the possibilities seemed endless. Then she remembered his financial situation and knew she couldn't saddle the man with two females. It wouldn't be fair to him, with the debts he would already be incurring. Besides, she was deceiving him about Sidney. She shook her head and sighed wistfully.

"What was that for?" Andrew asked quietly.

"Oh, nothing," she said, smiling tremulously.

"If you are ever in trouble or need a listening ear, Sharisse, I am available. I would welcome the opportunity to help you."

Sharisse nodded, a lump forming in her throat.

Andrew watched intently for a moment and then reached into a pocket and pulled out a draft on the Bank of England for twelve hundred and fifty pounds and silently extended it to her.

She took it, noting the amount and swallowed convulsively. Her questioning eyes raised to his warm ones. "Are you certain that this amount won't overextend you? I could take it over a period of time."

Andrew threw back his head and roared.

Sharisse looked at him wonderingly. What was so funny? She certainly didn't understand.

When he could contain himself, he took her hand. "I assure you that I am solvent and brought home a tidy bundle with me. You have no need to worry if the draft is good."

Sharisse was stung. "I had no such thoughts, sir. I was just trying to ease the burden."

Andrew's eyes softened and he rubbed the hand he still held. "I will never miss the money, darling, and I want you to know how touched I am by your generosity, but I am quite capable of affording the price." He raised her hand to his lips and kissed it.

Sharisse blushed. "Are you certain that this is what you want to pay?"

"I never do anything I don't want to. If I make up my mind to something, I never turn away from my goal."

Sharisse knew there was more to his words than she understood, but she couldn't catch his meaning, and bent her head in confusion. She quickly gained control and raised her chin. "Are you going to take Black Devil now?"

"No, as a matter of fact, my stables are not in good repair at the moment and I'd like to leave him here for a few days, if you don't mind."

A small hurricane with pigtails erupted into the room. "Rissy, is it all right . . ." Polly broke off as she saw Andrew. Her happy demeanor changed as she took in the tall figure. "What are you doing here?" she demanded.

"Polly!" Sharisse rebuked. "If your manners have deteriorated to this extent, I shall be forced to speak to your governess to see what can be done about it."

Polly's lower lip trembled at the cross tone. "I'm sorry. I just didn't expect to see Mr. Lindley so soon again."

"Polly, Mr. Lindley is the new Lord Brookfield, and I know you will wish to treat our new neighbor with all due respect."

Polly curtsyed and held out her hand, which Andrew took. "I'm pleased to make your acquaintance," she said in her most formal manner. Then Polly turned and ran from the room, muttering to herself, "We can't afford you."

Sharisse drew a sharp breath, for the words were clearly audible. "I don't know what gets into the child. Please forgive her, for she's been through an extremely trying few months."

"You mean with your father's death and your brother's injury?" Andrew waited, hoping that she would confide in him.

Sharisse spoke with great effort. "She's generally such a good child. It's just that this has been a bit much to bear. Mayhap I should be a little more stern, but I can't bring myself to do it." Sharisse felt herself drowning in sorrow for the child and for all that was not to be.

"You're to be commended on the way you're raising the child. She is delightful as she is. Surely, you wouldn't want to break her buoyant spirit?"

Sharisse regained her composure and turned the conversation. "I have to make a trip to London to see my solicitor. Would you be needing anything?"

"I have to make the trip myself. Perhaps you would allow me to drive you? We could take Polly and her governess if you'd like. It would give her a treat."

Sharisse weighed the possibilities. She would be able to see the solicitor alone and making the trip in his company would make the day enjoyable. "Thank you for your kind offer. Let us know when you plan to go and we'll endeavor to be ready."

She pulled her hands reluctantly from his and stood up. She felt a frantic desire to have met this man under different circumstances. Her deceit and his meager finances rendered the possibilities to the background.

"I will leave you now, and see about giving Black Devil some exercise. Once I have him behaving well enough to tolerate company, maybe you'll consent to ride out with me."

"The way you handle that horse, I expect to be invited out tomorrow."

"Done. I'll take the rough edges off him today and I'll be back tomorrow for your company. And plan on the next day for the trip up to London. If we start early and you haven't too many errands, we can be back before dark."

"There's nothing of the laggard about you." Her eyes twinkled at him. "I'll be ready," she promised.

She walked to the front door with him. Andrew winked broadly at her and then vaulted down the steps toward the stables.

Andrew gave orders for the horse to be saddled, and was soon prancing down the dirt path toward the tenant farms. Black Devil was champing at the bit, wanting to run, but Andrew held him with firm control.

This horse needed firm but gentle handling, just like his darling. Each needed time and patience, and he was a master at both. Sharisse promised to be every bit as much a handful as the horse under him and he had accepted the challenge.

He finally let the animal have its head, knowing that if he set a pattern of firm control first each session the horse would learn quickly who was master. He had said many times that women were like horses, but this particular woman threatened to break all of his carefully set rules.

Andrew found himself wanting to meet her every desire. He had always taught his paramours to accede to his wishes, but he had the distinct impression that Sharisse wouldn't dance to any man's tune.

He smiled brilliantly. Well, that young lady had met a force to be reckoned with. Andrew Lindley was not a man to rush his fences. He would gauge his timing carefully and set the pace to his liking.

As he reined into the stableyard, he dismounted and spoke a kind word to the stable hands. He had learned long before that a few words of praise paid better dividends than any amount of money. Still, Andrew pressed a coin into the man's hand.

"I harnessed yer 'orses, Lord Brookfield, when I saw ye comin' back up the road. The lad's out front with 'em."

"Miss Satterleigh is lucky to have you. Thank you, again."

Andrew strode to the front drive. The reflection pool seemed to beckon to him. He remembered when his pool had been full and used to feed the fish. Stepping up on the edge, he watched a fish feeding on the bottom. He was lost in thought, but old habits die hard and his instincts were alerted as he sensed someone behind him. As he whirled about, two small hands pushed him. As he lost his balance, he grabbed his assailant and the two of them toppled into the water. Andrew stood up immediately, holding a sputtering and coughing Polly. Her face was a study in consternation and surprise. He strode out of the pool and set her in front of him.

"What was the reason for this attack, Polly? What have I done that you don't approve of?" His voice was most intimidating, and struck fear into the little girl cowering before him.

Polly merely shook her head, too shocked to say anything. She was shaking violently.

"Polly," he tried in a calmer tone, "do you understand that

someone could have been seriously injured with that prank? I never mind a bit of fun, but this is beyond the line. It is no longer a game when it's possible to injure. I think it's time that you learned a valuable lesson. One that your sister hasn't seemed fit to teach."

With that he tucked her under one arm, her small derrière within convenient reach of his broad palm and proceeded to place three firm smacks where it would do the most good. Polly yelled for Sharisse, but Andrew held firm. When he was through he set her in front of him and recommended to Polly, "I trust that you will remember your manners in the future."

Sharisse heard her sister's cries through the open window and came running to see what the commotion was about. She saw the two dripping figures and Andrew just putting Polly down on her feet.

"Oh, Andrew. Polly's fallen in the pool and you jumped in to rescue her. How gallant of you."

"I didn't exactly jump in, darling." His clothes were sodden but his tone was quite dry.

"Polly, run into the house and get into some dry clothes. When you're finished wait for me in the study." Sharisse commanded in an angry tone.

At those ominous words, Polly ran for the house as if she were teasing the bull again and he were charging.

As she flew up the stairs her mind was churning. Sharisse was showing a decided liking for the dark, ugly stranger. He was the first one ever to paddle her backside, but the fact made her respect for him grow considerably. Nonetheless, Polly decided that he was not suitable husband material for Sharisse, for he didn't have enough money to keep her in style.

"Sharisse won't have to suffer too much because of me. I am almost positive that Sharisse will accept the first offer she gets just so that I have a decent home." Polly was incensed at the thought of Sharisse sacrificing herself. "Well, Sharisse, think again. I won't be treated like a baby. Besides I'm going to see that the ineligible suitors never get close enough to make an offer. I will do my duty to the family name, even if I have to resort to a little . . . what was that word Sharisse used the other day? . . . subterfuge. That's it. Even if I have to use subterfuge." The little girl's eyes sparkled with mischief.

CHAPTER SIX

Sharisse was arranging a vase of flowers in the breakfast room when Lord Brookfield was announced. She looked around in surprise, for it was only ten minutes past eight. "Good morning, Lord Brookfield. I didn't expect to see you quite so early."

"I don't care to hear that title on your lips. I wish you would call me Andrew. After all, we are neighbors and friends and I intend that we shall become much more."

Sharisse blushed furiously and poked flowers haphazardly into the vase. She had thought that she had her reactions under control, but this proved that she was susceptible to his charm. "I will call you Andrew if you will stop funning with me this way. I don't think I'm up to your weight."

Andrew started to say something and thought better of it. He turned the false start off with a sad cough. "Are you about ready for our ride?" He seemed skeptical.

After placing the last blossom into the vase and drying her hands, she turned to face him and cocked her head. "I can be ready in ten minutes, if you are so inclined."

"If you can be ready in ten minutes, darling, you are indeed a paragon." His lips twitched as he contemplated her saucy look.

"Why, thank you, Andrew. I deem that a nice compliment."

"I'll save the compliments until I see the proof," he returned, grinning.

"Very well then, I'll see you in ten minutes in the blue salon." She inclined her head regally and swept from the room.

Andrew's mirth erupted into laughter as she withdrew. He sauntered to the appointed room and found a wing-back chair to gain comfort while he waited. He studied his watch and shook his head. Not one damsel of his acquaintance could perform such a feat.

Sharisse rang the bell pull vigorously as she pulled off first one shoe and then the other.

Hannah hurried in, fussing. "What's all the rush? A body would think that you were stepping out with one of those town beaux."

"I engaged Lord Brookfield in a wager, Hannah, and I must be ready to ride in eight more minutes." Sharisse grinned and her eyes sparkled as she spoke and turned her back to the maid.

"I might think that your head had been turned, if I didn't know better."

To Sharisse it was a sobering thought. If she were that transparent, what would Andrew think? She stopped her reflections and she busied herself with her toilette, picked out a hat, and ran for the stairs.

"As you see, I didn't quite have time to put on my bonnet but I am within the required time." She curtsyed pertly and then placed the crisp bowler on her auburn curls with no attempt to set it at the most becoming angle.

"I am impressed." He put out his arm and asked, "May I?"

Sharisse took the proffered arm and strolled out to the stables with him.

"Tell me about your stay in India. I would like to know a little bit about what you did."

Andrew described the bazaars, the shipping and trading business, and gave her a bit of detail about the countinghouses.

"Are you saying that you were a clerk in the countinghouses for your entire stay?"

"No, I diversified my interests after a few years. I found that the life suited me and was, on the whole, quite good to me. I invested my savings in a partnership with a trader and turned a tidy profit."

He spoke so matter-of-factly that Sharisse mistook his modesty for an apology that he hadn't come home a nabob. It gave her pause for thought. It had occurred to her that if the man had made his fortune in India, he would have been able to restore Brookfield Hall and support her and Polly in the manner which they had been accustomed. She sighed audibly.

"What was that for?" he inquired.

"I was just thinking how much difference money or lack of it can make to one's life."

"Don't worry yourself unduly about money, sweetheart. Things have a way of turning out for the best. Take me, for instance. I don't regret my time in India one whit. My father actually did me a favor by making me accept some responsibility for myself and learn how to handle what finances were at my disposal."

Sharisse gave him a tremulous smile and nodded.

They conversed lightly as they waited for Firefly to be saddled. Sharisse peeked up at Andrew from under her long lashes and fluttered them provocatively when he made a comment about her lack of undesirable feminine tricks. They both laughed.

When Firefly was brought out, Andrew put his hands around her small waist and lifted her into the saddle with one smooth movement.

"Andrew! Lord Brookfield!"

He merely smiled, not in the least contrite for his unorthodox assistance. It was plain that he was enjoying himself immensely.

Andrew controlled Black Devil with such ease that Sharisse wondered if he had almost run the animal into the ground before he'd come around to the front door.

"Did you put Black Devil through his paces or is it that he knows he can't outmaneuver you?" she inquired musingly.

"Why, it's my superior horsemanship, of course." He grinned and then added, "And of course I did let him have his head for a stretch."

Sharisse grinned. "You're a complete hand."

They left the courtyard with an air of comradery, heading for the Home Wood.

Polly looked out her bedchamber window and saw the duo conversing easily. There was no doubt in her mind that her sister was showing a decided partiality for the dark-skinned stranger. This was a first, and Polly thought that she knew the reason. "Well, I'll find some way to stop him."

Polly tabled her contemplation of Andrew's next incident when her stomach growled. "Cook may have something to hold me until nuncheon."

The door to the kitchen was open and as Polly approached it she could hear cook's voice talking to her young assistant.

"Upon my word, Millie. That black heathen is coming here just like he was a single man."

"Ee, yer mean he's married?" Horror was plain in Millie's voice. "And he's a courting our Miss Sharisse?"

Cook suddenly swung around, having heard or sensed Polly. "Well now, and what are ye up to?"

Polly pretended she hadn't heard the conversation. "Just looking for a biscuit waiting around for me."

Cook reached into a large stone jar and pulled out two large sugar biscuits. "Here ye are but if ye don't eat yer nuncheon, don't blame me."

Polly took them and thanked cook, her eyes turning to Millie to see what the assistant was doing. She decided that the disclosure was at an end. "I'm going to see if the dogs want to go for a run." Polly had much to ponder as she made her way to the stables.

"Well, I'm guessing that he's married, but I really don't know for certain. All I know is what I heard from the postman in town. He says that Andrew Lindley ran away with some lady when he was nineteen and he'd heard that they had left the country, so he thought that they had got married. I never did hear if she died or what, so it's my belief that he's married, till I hear differently."

"I think ye're probably right. Never 'ave I 'eard such goin's on."

Polly let the dogs out and headed toward the meandering stream past the park. It was a favorite hideout of hers. The little girl had much to ponder as the dogs frolicked in the water. Polly picked a blade of grass and chewed it thoughtfully. Sharisse was in for quite a shock. The question was how to broach the subject.

She knew for a fact that Sharisse wouldn't be pleased with the tale and that Sharisse would probably give her a trimming for listening to such talk, but possibly it would do the trick.

Sharisse watched as Andrew cantered Black Devil toward the creek bank without a check in his speed. She slowed up to appreciate the superb horsemanship. Andrew maneuvered the animal to just the spot he wanted and signaled the horse to make the jump with a slight lifting of the reins and a shift of his weight. Man and beast sailed over the creek and landed well past the eroded bank. Andrew patted the horse's neck and uttered soothing words.

He then turned to Sharisse and waited for her to cross.

Sharisse chose a spot that wasn't quite so treacherous and put Firefly to the test. Firefly's leap wasn't so spectacular, but it was creditable.

"Jolly good," praised Andrew as Sharisse rode up.

"I can see that you are perfectly happy with your new hunter, Andrew. The two of you seem as one. I could almost believe that this isn't the animal I sold you two days ago."

"Are you sorry now that you let him go?" The eyebrows quirked and he gave her an amused smile.

"No. There's no one but Sidney who could have even attempted to ride him, and I believe that Black Devil could have been fashioned just for you."

"Thank you, darling. I will hold that as a high compliment."

"Andrew, I thought that you agreed to stop funning with me."

"But, darling, I thought you realized. I'm not funning. I'm perfectly serious." He reached over and ran a finger lightly down her cheek.

Sharisse kicked Firefly lightly in the flanks and as the mare surged forward, she called, "I'll race you." She knew that she had a good start and that the track through the woods wouldn't allow him to pass her for some time.

Andrew's tender smile vanished as Sharisse disappeared around the bend in the path. "Stubborn darling. She just can't quite accept the challenge, but I will yet break her to bridle before the game is over." With that he put a light spur to Black Devil and they were soon thundering up the path.

Andrew soon caught sight of his quarry but knew just as she did that he couldn't hope to pass her until they reached the meadow. He bided his time, waiting patiently for the right moment. When the meadow appeared at the edge of the wood, he spurred his mount and gave a yell. The horse responded immediately and closed the distance between the contestants.

Sharisse watched as he pulled alongside, a somewhat grim look on his face. Pulling Firefly to an easy stop, she said pertly, "I won," and waited for the storm to break.

"That depends on what you expected to win. If it was a spanking for such irresponsible behavior, I'll be most happy to oblige you. If it's a kiss for being able to control your horse through that treacherous course, I might even accommodate you, but if you expect me to concede that you are a better horseman, think again." He waited expectantly for her answer.

Sharisse alternately blushed and fumed. Her foot tapped furiously in its stirrup. Finally, a smile erupted. "I don't like any of your choices, but I accept the words of praise graciously. Thank you."

"You are a courageous young lady, darling, but I wish that you would let me help you. I can, you know."

Sharisse was aware that the conversation had taken a sudden turn and was pressed for an answer. She took refuge in deliberately misunderstanding him. "I am perfectly capable of handling Firefly, but thank you for your offer."

Andrew smiled enigmatically. "Just remember my offer, darling. I'm always available to help you."

Polly waited for Sharisse outside her bedchamber while she changed out of her riding habit. She knew that she must impart her news before Sharisse went down to oversee the dinner arrangements or she would have to wait until bedtime to get her alone again.

As the door opened, Polly stepped into her sister's path and pulled at the skirt of her jonquil day gown.

Sharisse gave Polly a tender smile and asked, "What is it, Polly, that you must waylay me in the hall?"

"Will you come into the study for a moment and talk to me?" She tugged on Sharisse's hand and looked stealthily around.

When they reached the room, after a deal of mystery, Sharisse grew slightly impatient. "Polly, what is it that's so secret?"

"I know that you don't like me to listen to servants' gossip, but I couldn't help overhearing this."

"Polly, I don't want you to repeat tales that probably aren't true. We've had several discussions on this head already."

"But, Rissy, this one said that Lord Brookfield is married," Polly blurted out quickly.

"What?" breathed Sharisse uncomprehendingly. She shook her head in bewilderment. Andrew was clearly trying to fix his interest with her. She knew him to be a man of honor. He wouldn't do such a thing unless he were single. It didn't make sense. "Polly, tell me what you heard and who said it."

"I heard cook telling Millie about it. Cook said that she heard it straight from the postmaster and you know that he hears everything that goes on in the village."

Sharisse bent down to Polly and placed a hand on each shoulder. "Polly, I know this may seem hard to understand for a little girl, but rumors aren't always true. We have talked about it many times. Remember the gossip about Farmer Talbot? That proved to be a bunch of nonsense started by a couple of angry neighbors."

Polly got into the spirit of the thing and recalled several other instances when the gossips had gotten the story mixed up, but when she was done she looked up at Sharisse with mournful eyes. "But, Sharisse, I don't like him. He's too mean to me." Polly knew that wasn't strictly true, realizing that Lord Brookfield had had good cause for spanking her, but she wanted Sharisse to be happy in her marriage and she just couldn't see that the dark, gruff stranger was the right man for her sister.

Sharisse swallowed tears and held her head up to channel them down the back of her throat instead of down her cheeks. When she could gain control again, she looked back at Polly. "I know that you don't like him, precious, but sometimes, we don't understand what's best for us when we're your age. Let me promise you this. I will look about London for all eligible candidates before coming to any decision. And as for the rumor, we'll just wait and see."

CHAPTER SEVEN

The next morning Sharisse was reviewing menus for the day while her mind still wrestled with the problem of whether or not to journey to London with Andrew. If the rumor were true, she would be committing a serious faux pas, but she had never credited servants' gossip, so what was her problem? Andrew was a man of honor and she couldn't imagine him trying to fix his interest if he were married, so why was she so fidgety?

Cook saw the worry lines about her mistress's face. "Miss Sharisse, don't you care for the roast duck with orange sauce for dinner?"

Sharisse was still pondering Andrew's supposed marriage and spoke absently. "Fudge!"

"You want fudge for dessert? That's not a problem, but what would you rather have for the main course? A braise of beef with onion garnish?"

Sharisse muttered under her breath, "If he's been toying with me, I'll fix his goose."

"Goose is a very good choice. Even better than the duck." The woman finished rolling out a pie crust and turned to face Sharisse. "What are we celebrating?" Cook tried in vain to remember if Sharisse had told her of some important event. Noting her mistress was plainly distracted, she decided that it was best not to repeat the question.

Sharisse roused herself from her thoughts as she perceived cook studying her intensely. "I was just worrying about my trip to London today. Set dinner back until nine o'clock. I know that seems quite *ton*ish, but I don't believe that I'll be back early."

"How many should I plan on for dinner?"

"Did I give you the impression we were having guests?"

"Miss Sharisse, you asked to have goose for dinner tonight," complained the faithful servant.

"Did I? My thoughts must have been on something else." Sharisse laughed and tried to turn the subject, but two telltale spots of color rose to her cheeks as she remembered what she'd said.

"Françoise, the roast duck with orange sauce will be wonderful. I'll look forward to it all the way home." With that she went off in search of Simms.

When she heard carriage wheels, she knew that the Meadows was receiving morning callers. The noise of a fairly loud altercation brought Sharisse to the great hall in a rush. Sharisse found Simms looking as if he had just heard that Sidney had died, and as he perceived her, he regarded her with pleading eyes.

She had never in all her days seen Simms at a loss. One could always count on him. He was like the local vicar. One could always set his watch by the man, he was so predictable.

Sharisse studied the new arrivals dispassionately to see what had caused the old man's loss of objectivity. The full-figured woman now silent, dressed in the latest fashion stood regally in the hall while her daughter waited meekly. The woman's puce morning gown was of the Empress Josephine style and sported several shades of flowers and ribbons.

Sharisse could be trusted to depress pretensions in the most valued guest and her slow appraisal had its effect on the young lady, almost hiding in her mother's wake. Her chin rose a fraction as she was the object of her girl's pity. Sharisse usually made instant decisions about others and she could tell without hearing the pair that the daughter would do just as her mother bid her, even though she must be all of nineteen. Sharisse noted the rounded abdomen protruding beneath her jonquil gown and waited grimly for the next announcement.

The older woman's bosom heaved as she started to speak.

"Miss Sharisse Satterleigh? But I need not ask. Of course you are Sir Sidney's sister. The likeness is remarkable."

"I'm afraid I didn't catch your name," Sharisse said with a cool but formal smile, extending her hand.

"I am Mrs. Moffat," the woman replied, as if that should explain everything.

"I'm afraid that I don't recognize the name." Sharisse noted the tentative smile on the girl's face and decided that she might be able to make a friend of her if she could be gotten away from her mother's influence.

"Oh dear, I might have guessed it. You have never received a letter from your brother. When I found that no notice had been sent to the *Gazette,* I took care of it post haste."

Mrs. Moffat smiled triumphantly at her achievement, though Sharisse couldn't have said what it was.

"I see," murmured Sharisse, not making the disclosure the slightest bit easy.

"How naughty of that dear boy. I've brought you a present. Miss Satterleigh, may I present Lady Margaret Satterleigh."

Sharisse's first reaction was denial, but there would be time for that later if it proved to be a hoax. She wondered then if the duo had heard of Sidney's death. She gestured the mother and daughter to the blue salon and rang the pull. "The mail is very poor from India and somehow we've missed your news. I'm pleased to welcome you to the Meadows."

"Simms, have Mrs. Brown prepare rooms for Mrs. Moffat and Lady Satterleigh."

The old man nodded and thrust his shoulders back. "Very good, miss." There could be no doubt where his loyalty would lie.

Underfootmen were still bringing in handboxes, but Sharisse ignored the hubbub.

"Have you come straight from India? I didn't know there was another ship due." The packet usually only came every month or two.

Mrs. Moffat tittered. "Dear Sidney desired us to leave some time ago, as Margaret is increasing and he didn't think the climate was good for her. He plans to sell out and come home as soon as possible." The abrasive woman was reveling in her tale. "We sent to Scotland to our home to rest and collect our things."

Sharisse applauded herself for accepting the news so calmly. "May I ask what made you attempt such a harsh journey to India?"

"We went to visit my brother, Major Bentworth, for a short time. Then Margaret met Sidney and he swept her off her feet."

Sharisse would have the solicitor check the validity of the claim, but in the interval she'd make the best of the situation. It was not like Sidney at all to let someone else break such news. He was a man of character and principle. If it were possible, he would have at the very least written. It therefore seemed that he had either been stricken down before he had been able to write or that the tale was just that. "How convenient for you." Sharisse couldn't stop the cutting remark.

Mrs. Brown hurried into the blue salon followed by Mary Potts, the old nurse.

"Come along with me, Yer Ladyship. I know just what you need," the nurse crooned with a welcoming grin. It was plain to see the old woman was delighted to have something to do again. Margaret followed gratefully, the long journey showing in her walk.

Mrs. Moffat sniffed at the interchange, but didn't deign to comment.

"Mrs. Moffat, this is my housekeeper, Mrs. Brown. I will leave you in her hands while I attend to the details of arranging for your stay. Mrs. Brown, I think that our guest would be happy in the corner tower." She didn't add, away from all the bustle.

The housekeeper gave her mistress a knowing look that spoke volumes. She was happy to see a division of the opposing forces at the outset.

Sharisse took refuge in her most polite tone. "I hope you'll be very happy with us during your stay."

The old matron smiled benignly at Sharisse, believing she had received all the respect she and her offspring were due.

When they had ascended the stairs, Sharisse drew an audible breath of relief. The interchange had taken considerable time, and it had been and would continue to be a test of her manners to be civil to the woman.

Polly was playing outside when Andrew drove up. He waved at her and continued on to the stables to leave his team until Sharisse was ready to go. His lip was pressed between his teeth as he noted Polly's dirty smock and flyaway pigtails. It wasn't like Sharisse to let Polly go to town in that condition. It gave him pause for thought.

Simms answered the door unusually quickly, and as Andrew entered, he noted the pile of luggage being removed from the great hall. Arching an eyebrow at the old servant, he was about to query the man when Sharisse rushed forward to greet him enthusiastically.

"Oh, Andrew, my good friend." It was quite plain that he was a welcome distraction. "As you can see we are at sixes and sevens. It seems that my brother married a few months ago and forgot to write us about it. His bride and her mama have just arrived."

Andrew clasped her hands and smiled warmly at her. "I seem to recall he was keeping company with a young lady. What may I do to help you?"

Sharisse refused to believe that if Andrew were already married he would show such partiality for her company. She had assessed him to be a man of honor and saw no reason to change her mind. "This changed my plans considerably. I won't be able to go to London today. Also, my sister-in-law is increasing and so we must take special care of her." Her eyes begged for understanding. "She may produce an heir," she murmured absently, more to herself than to Andrew.

A curious expression sat on his face for a few seconds before he smiled. Here was confirmation of his suspicions that the letter she had received had indeed told of Sidney's death. He raised her hand to his lips. "I am yours to command. Only tell me how I may be able to ease the burden, and I will assist you in any way."

"Andrew, how can you perceive that receiving a new sister is a burden? However, I do wish that Sidney had taken the time to write." Her brow wrinkled in distress.

Andrew smoothed the brow and consoled her. "The men are very busy while they're on patrol. Sometimes they are out for months at a time."

"Thank you, that's what I wanted to hear. The news came as quite a shock, and I'm pleased to think that there's a logical explanation for the lack of notice. Will you stay and have a cup of tea with me? I feel the need of a stimulant." And your company, she added silently.

He hesitated and then allowed himself to be led into the morning room. After she had rung for tea, he seated her with great care in one of the comfortable wing-back chairs.

Her eyes asked the old butler a question, and as he placed the tray carefully near her, he answered in a voice carefully devoid of emotion, "Mrs. Moffat sent down word she would join you in a cup directly."

Sharisse knew immediately that there was already trouble with her guests.

At the name, Andrew's eyebrows rose a fraction of an inch, but he didn't comment.

At that moment Mrs. Moffat sailed regally into the room with the air of conferring a favor on the assembled company. Andrew uncoiled his length and stood to greet her.

Sharisse didn't quite have time to introduce them before Mrs. Moffat cut her short. "We have met in India." Her tone was not cordial but neither was it hostile.

The greeting struck Sharisse as unusual. It seemed that her guest didn't quite know what to make of Andrew. "Lord Brookfield is my neighbor, Mrs. Moffat."

The woman's comment was non sequitur. "Dear Margaret is tired after the journey, and your nurse has taken over. I don't think that the woman will do. Already she's exerting a good deal of influence on my child and I'm not certain that I like her attitude. I think I may have to dismiss her." She spoke quite positively and took the cup Sharisse was handing her.

Sharisse smiled tightly at the woman. "I'm afraid you can't do that, Mrs. Moffat. Nurse is an institution at the Meadows and Sidney won't stand for having his own nurse dismissed."

She managed to speak gently, but Andrew noted the fire in her eyes, and his lips curled in amusement.

Mrs. Moffat was not to be denied, and merely let the matter rest for the while. "We'll see. It's early days yet, but I know for a fact that Margaret will be wanting to replace several of the old servants with smarter, younger ones. However, that's a subject for another day."

Sharisse could only be thankful that before Sidney had left for India he'd had Mr. Critchfield draw up some kind of legal document that gave her absolute control while he was away. It was almost as if he had foreseen the need. She had always been close to Sidney and somehow she had usually known when he was hurt. She just felt it. She didn't know why, she just did. Now that her brain was functioning again, after the shock of being told he was dead, she had the nagging feeling that he was calling to her. Dead people didn't call others, did they? She set aside her reflections and addressed the woman.

"Mrs. Moffat, I believe that you're right. This isn't the time for such a discussion. You may want to take it up with Mr. Critchfield, our family solicitor, after you have given him Margaret's marriage lines."

Andrew grinned silently and winked. Sharisse took a deep breath and launched her second volley. "I hate to be the bearer of sad news, but perhaps you haven't heard that Sidney was gravely wounded in some sort of tribal unrest. He was sent to Paris to a renowned surgeon. He is not conscious yet and won't be expected to make a recovery for some time." Sharisse's knuckles whitened on the arms of her chair as she uttered the prevarications.

Andrew rose to take his leave. "I must be excused. You ladies have much on your minds." He bowed briefly to Mrs. Moffat and walked from the room.

Sharisse followed him to the door where he turned and whispered, "The old busybody. You score excellent marks on your first battle of wills. If you need help, remember I'm willing."

Polly came trotting into the great hall looking like a thundercloud. She stopped when she saw Andrew. "Why are you here?" she demanded indignantly.

Andrew bent down to the child. "Now, Polly, what have I done to raise your ire?"

"Polly, what's happened to your manners? Lord Brookfield has called to take us to London and I've had to decline."

At these words Polly's face cleared. "I beg your pardon," she chimed sweetly, thinking that her wishes had been acceded to. "Sharisse, cook told me that Sidney's wife and mama-in-law are here."

"Yes, indeed. Come in to the drawing room and meet Mrs. Moffat." She held out her hand to Andrew. "Thank you for everything."

Andrew raised her hand to his lips, brushing it slightly.

Sharisse turned determinedly and marched Polly into the battleground. "Mrs. Moffat, this is my sister, Polly. Polly, this is Sidney's new mama-in-law, Mrs. Moffat."

The gruff woman looked Polly up and down with a distinct look of disapproval on her angular features, taking note of the dirty pinafore, rumpled dress, dirty face, and flyaway braids. "I've heard about you and it would seem to be true. You stand in need of some strong discipline."

Polly's temper wasn't any better than her sister's and she hadn't had the years of practice disguising it. She scowled ferociously. "You have no say over me."

Sharisse put a restraining hand on Polly's shoulder, and Polly turned to her sister and murmured, "Well, she hasn't." Then she streaked out the door after the briefest curtsy.

Balked of her prey, Mrs. Moffat turned back to Sharisse. "I can't understand why you received word about Sidney's wounds before we did. After all, the colonel knew of his marriage to my daughter."

"Perhaps you left a Scottish address and your letter has gone there." If, indeed, there were a second letter, which seemed quite possible, then Sharisse could find herself in a barrel of pickles. Well, she decided morosely, she'd have to cross that moat if and when the time came. There was no use speculating on it at the moment.

If that domineering woman meant to go on as she'd started, the sooner Polly and she left the Meadows, the better. First, she must get to London and sound out Mr. Critchfield. Then she could map out her campaign.

"I suppose that it is entirely possible. Now tell me why that man is running tame in this house." Her lips were firmed to a straight line, her back rigid with disapproval. "You must know that he is a rake. It won't do for my Margaret to be associated with the like. I must ask you to forbid him the house."

Sharisse who had been thinking of keeping him away until she could be certain that he wasn't married, came rushing to his defense. "He has been most helpful to me in my distress over my brother. I find him a very pleasant gentleman. I'm afraid that even for you I won't deny myself the pleasure of his company."

A flame in Mrs. Moffat's eyes told Sharisse that she hadn't heard the last of this, even though she had managed to win the first skirmish.

On the pretext that she had work to do, she left Mrs. Moffat to her own devices. She found herself completely out of charity with her guest but resolved to put a bridle on her emotions. There were more important matters to settle. She headed for the housekeeper to settle the issues raised by the additions to the household.

She found Mrs. Brown with linen sorted into two piles. At Sharisse's appearance Mrs. Brown gave her a wide smile. "Ee, love, but I'm that glad to see ye. I put Mrs. Moffat in the turret room at the end of the east hall, as you suggested, but I think that she'd be better in the dungeon."

"We do have an image to keep up at the Meadows, and I see no reason to change that now." Sharisse's jaw inched upward and her tone was sharper than usual. She threw up her hands and laughed. "Mrs. Brown, I always trust your judgment. Don't let my grumpiness upset you."

"Now Miss Margaret will do nicely by the nursery." As the words left her mouth, Sharisse heard raised voices in the kitchen.

She marched in to see cook and Polly ranged on one side of the table and Mrs. Moffat on the other.

Cook pointed a wooden spoon at Mrs. Moffat. "That woman is trying to stir up trouble."

Mrs. Moffat rounded on her new target. "I don't know what kind of house you think to run here, but I tell you I won't have it. As soon as Margaret comes down she'll give orders here and all the unsatisfactory servants can be turned off."

Polly cut in. "Sharisse, I didn't do anything, nor did cook. Mrs. Moffat came down here and tried to tell cook how to prepare the duck for dinner. Then my turtle just happened to fall out of my pocket and she saw it and thought it was a mouse and began screaming."

Sharisse was quite needle-witted and saw at a glance that Mrs. Moffat had tried to run roughshod over cook and, since cook was unable to tell a guest to mind her business, Polly had taken up the cudgels. "Mrs. Moffat, you must excuse Polly. She doesn't normally carry her turtle about the house, but she is only a child. I'm sorry that you had such a bad experience. Perhaps part of it is the fact that you've had a tiring day. Why don't you rest awhile before dinner? Moreover, we wouldn't want Margaret to be upset, would we?"

With those words, Mrs. Moffat allowed herself to be led away.

Cook winked at Polly and reached for two freshly baked maid-of-honors, handing one to the little girl. Both grinned silently as they munched their treat.

CHAPTER EIGHT

Sharisse woke with a sense of foreboding. Margaret was a biddable girl and would have probably made Sidney just the sort of wife he needed, and he would have separated his bride from his mama-in-law quite efficiently at the start. But now that he wouldn't be here to do that, Sharisse was involved in an intolerable situation. It was true that Sidney had signed papers turning complete management of the estate over to her, but, drat it, with his death the estate would pass out of her hands.

She rolled over and sighed. Things couldn't be worse unless Margaret had a girl, and then when she "received" word that Sidney died, the search for an heir would begin. Not for the first time did she mentally castigate the system. Somehow it didn't seem quite fair.

Margaret would have need of her mother's support when Sharisse broke her news, and she was bound, and it wouldn't be until several months after the baby was born. After all, whom was she withholding from the succession? No one—at least no one until Margaret had a girl.

Sharisse threw the covers back with a resolve to show Margaret the house today and to send a message to ask Belinda, her childhood friend and neighbor, now Lady Winchley, if she would like to accompany her to London.

As she was donning the last of her petticoats, in flew Polly. "Rissy, what are we going to do? I'm sorry, but I can't abide that woman. She thinks she's in charge of everyone and everything." Polly's normal dimpled smile was drooping into a fierce scowl.

When Sharisse noticed that Polly was wearing her favorite red dress and white pinafore, she knew that the day indeed portended disaster. Polly was constantly telling Sharisse that this particular outfit made her feel good. Evidently the child needed reassurance. Sharisse gathered her close.

"Lambie, we've got a problem, but I'm trying to resolve it. I'm planning a day in London to see Mr. Critchfield. Perhaps he can tell me something that might be of help."

The little girl tightened her thin arms about Sharisse's neck and buried her head in her sister's hair. "You're not going to tell him about the letter?" she whispered dramatically.

"No, I plan to get as much information as I can without telling anything of importance, and believe me, with Mr. Critchfield being such a pattern card of rectitude, I am going to find myself in the briars if I'm not careful."

"You haven't given up the idea of a rich husband?" Polly raised tear-splashed eyes to Sharisse's earnest ones.

"I'm afraid I can't think of a better plan, lambie." A curious expression crossed her face. "He doesn't necessarily have to be rich—just comfortable enough to provide for us." She gave her sister a kiss and a tweak on the nose. "Come on now, brat, give me a smile."

Polly's scowl increased. "Does that mean you might consider Lord Brookfield? He seems to be in your company often but he doesn't look as if he could afford to buy our dresses, much less our living."

Sharisse chuckled. "In the first place, he's merely being neighborly, as he knew Sidney. Second, I doubt if he has marriage in his mind." The words hurt to say, but until she'd had time to sort that tale through, she'd play least seen, soonest forgot.

"You mean you think he might offer you a carte blanche?" inquired Polly interestedly.

"Polly!" Sharisse almost shrieked. "Where do you hear such talk? I must speak to Miss Roberts immediately. If the servants have been talking like that within your hearing, I'm going to have some plain speaking with them."

Polly hung her head in mock abashment, but only until one dimple peeked out. "I just happened to hear them talking about all Lord Brookfield's women and cook said carte blanche and Milly didn't know what it meant. I listened while she said."

Sharisse shook her head. It was difficult at best to keep one step ahead of this precocious youngster. She tried another tack. "Promise me that today you'll not get into Mrs. Moffat's bad graces. We have enough on our dish without having to keep soothing her disordered senses."

"I don't think she likes children." Polly folded her arms and waited for a comment.

"Nonsense! You just got off to a bad start. It'll be better today, you'll see." She hoped she sounded more confident than she felt. And if Andrew decided to run over again today and have a turnup with Mrs. Moffat, she'd be at *point non plus*. Giving Polly another quick hug, she shooed her out the door.

When Sharisse entered the breakfast room a few minutes later, she found Mrs. Moffat there ahead of her, apparently examining the table setting. Her eyes were as hard as two bits of coal as she picked up a plate and examined it. She looked up as Sharisse appeared and charged at once.

"Do you realize that the servants have set the breakfast table with good Wedgwood? These are too valuable to use in the morning." The woman's tone was one that might be used to lecture an ignorant country girl.

Sharisse took a steadying breath. "Mrs. Moffat, the Satterleighs have used these plates for breakfast for years on end. It's a tradition with us. We use our Spode for dinner."

"Ah well, this will change when Margaret takes charge. There will be quite a few different goings-on here."

Sharisse felt the waves of heat rising upward from her clenched fingers. Trying to ignore the direct rudeness, she inquired, "Is Margaret coming down this morning?"

"I wanted her to stay in bed, but your nurse had other ideas and Margaret is listening to her. Something has to be done about that woman."

Polly's countenance showed a quiet anger, but she merely watched the way Sharisse stood up to Mrs. Moffat.

Before Sharisse could reply, Margaret came shyly into the room, nurse following in her wake.

"There you are, my lady. Now have a good breakfast. It'll do you and the baby good. Afterwards we'll see what Miss Sharisse has planned for you." With that nurse nodded and took herself off.

Margaret greeted her mother and new relatives in a soft voice, as she seated herself on her new sister-in-law's right.

Mrs. Moffat took up the cudgels. "Now this won't do, Margaret. You should sit at the head of the table. You are now the mistress of this house." She glared at Sharisse.

Margaret was in an agony of embarrassment, and, seeing it, Sharisse felt sorry for the girl. "Of course, you are exactly right. I didn't think of it." She stood as she spoke.

Margaret, her face becomingly flushed, stammered prettily that she wouldn't hear of it.

It was plain that this didn't suit Mrs. Moffat. Her small mouth was set in a grim line but she made no retort.

"At breakfast we help ourselves from the sideboard. Please select what you'd like. If there's something missing you prefer, you have just to ask and I'll have cook send it up."

Mrs. Moffat pushed her chair back and made her way to the sideboard. She allowed Margaret to precede her and made a fuss that she try to eat something to keep up her strength. As she lifted one lid the smell of fresh bacon wafted upward and permeated the room. Another dish had broiled fish, while others contained ham, porridge, toast, crumpets, scrambled eggs, and a variety of pastries.

The selection was quite large, but Mrs. Moffat sniffed deprecatingly at most of the choices. Most of the others were seated when the woman finally settled on ham and eggs.

Polly was left to take her turn. Just as she ladled out her first scoop of porridge, Mrs. Moffat began to screech. Polly's smile broadened dramatically for a moment and then she transformed her face into the angelic smile Sharisse knew so well. She sat down interestedly as Sharisse and Margaret tried to quiet the woman.

"Mrs. Moffat, stop this instant!"

"Mama, please be still."

Mrs. Moffat picked up a sharp thistle and waved it about. "This is what she did. The wretched girl. I know this is her doing." Her complexion was mottled with anger. "And as for you, young lady, you need to be taught how to behave. I shall undertake that task with pleasure."

Margaret shrank in her chair, her lips trembling, but Sharisse didn't notice, for she was busy holding her churning temper. "Mrs. Moffat! I shall see to Polly." She turned to her sister with a furious glance. "That was a very childish prank. Apologize immediately."

Polly hung her head and choked out the words. Thereafter the breakfast was consumed in a strained silence. Sharisse and Margaret exchanged speaking looks.

As the meal came to a close, Mrs. Moffat broke the silence, seeing the need to retrieve her position. "My dear Miss Satterleigh, it seems we've gotten off to a poor start. I'd like to try to begin again. Please call me Albinia." She had pasted what passed for a smile on her face, but her eyes were still hard and calculating.

Sharisse swallowed a stinging retort and agreed. Only her long training as a hostess enabled her to be civil to the woman. She turned to Margaret. "Do you feel up to going over the house to acquaint yourself with it? We'll interview cook and our housekeeper, Mrs. Brown."

For the first time Margaret showed some animation. A soft smile curved her lips. "I'd like that. I want to know just how you do things and what Sidney likes, so when he gets home I can please him."

This ingenuous speech almost choked Sharisse. The pain was so deep her breath was short. To cover the lapse she directed a stern look at Polly. "Go to your room and think about your behavior until I come to speak with you."

The little girl didn't offer an answer, and meekly made for the door, her head hanging.

The servants had lined up at the door to the morning room

to give Margaret a warm welcome and a respectful curtsy or bow. Mrs. Moffat watched benevolently over the proceedings, but for her part received only bare civility.

Sharisse interpreted the action quickly. Margaret was to become one of the family, but Mrs. Moffat would get short shrift.

Sharisse led her new sister-in-law through the various parlors and sitting rooms and then returned to the main floor, where they found nurse bustling about in the small morning room, making it comfortable for Margaret. The old servant had pulled up an easy chair and footstool near the large window so Margaret could have a view of the gardens. "Now, love, you've had enough exercise for a bit. It's time to have some milk."

Simms appeared magically with the required drink and nurse fussed over her new charge with a deal of cajoling.

Sharisse saw that her guests were comfortably established before making her way to Polly.

"Polly, I know that Mrs. Moffat would try the patience of all the saints put together, but somehow we must contrive until I can solve our problems. Do you think you can resist playing tricks on her?"

Polly set her doll down carefully. "Each time I try, she criticizes us or the way we do things."

"You be on your best behavior and I'll endeavor to free us of this coil as quickly as possible." She stood up. "I'm going to ride over to Winchley and see if Lady Winchley would like to go to London with us. If you'll stay in your room, you'll be spared that woman's nasty tongue."

Polly grinned. She understood that was supposed to be her punishment, but both girls knew that Polly's favorite pastime was playing with her dolls and her tea set.

"That I promise." She gave Sharisse a saucy smirk. "But why don't we take Timothy coachman and go ourselves?"

"I thought we'd better leave the carriage and Timothy at Margaret's disposal. After all, she has more right to it than I at present."

"You're too nice and if you don't watch out you'll catch cold at that."

"Polly! Where do you get those cant expressions? A lady doesn't use such language."

"I've already been told by Mrs. Moffat that I'm no such thing."

Sharisse shook her head. Polly was never backward with a retort.

"I'll come straight up here as soon as I return."

A few minutes later she was in the stableyard, calling for her mare. She had just fastened her gloves when Cowley led the frisky mare from the barn.

"Ee, Miss Sharisse, she be a handful this morn. She's missed her run." There was a slight accusation in his voice.

Sharisse nodded, but her eyes glistened as she anticipated the treat she'd awarded herself for holding her temper.

One of the young stable hands ran out to make a hand for her and she sprang lightly into the saddle. Whispering assurances to the animal, she gave Cowley the signal to stand away. The horse was indeed fresh and playful, but Sharisse gathered the reins firmly and turned toward Winchley.

It was a typical English country morning. The sun cast a golden glow on the lush green fields and warmed everything it touched. There was no breeze but the air smelled fresh and clean. Sharisse welcomed the mare's desire to run and at the end of the lane let her have her head. A trilling laugh escaped her lips and she gave herself over to the pleasure of skillfully guiding the mare through the fields and over the various hedges and fences.

When Sharisse found that she was singing under her breath, she knew she had better take time for herself more often. She hadn't found the desire to sing since the letter had come.

She gathered herself to make the hardest jump of the morning as she saw the south hedgerow appear. As she made her approach she could hear another set of thundering hoofbeats. Her attention remained focused on the jump. Sharisse held her mount in until the very last second and then lifted the reins to signal the jump. Timing was critical, for there was a bit of a ditch on the other side that must be cleared. For a second the world was quiet and then the horse grunted as she gained the hillside below and the pounding hoofs continued. Sharisse began to pull up as she discerned Andrew beside her.

"And now, my precious, perhaps you will tell me why you have frightened me so badly?" His visage was clouded and his voice was stern.

"I've been over this land since I could sit a saddle. You've naught to be concerned about for me." Her chin rose a fraction and her eyes glittered.

Andrew's frown disappeared and his eyes warmed as he took in her flushed face and defiance. "I took careful note of your horsemanship. You'll do quite nicely, but until I saw your style I was concerned. A lesser rider could have broken her neck."

"My, I do believe that buried under the censure was a compliment. Tell me, were you seeking me or are you just out for a morning ride?"

"I asked Cowley which way you went, having arrived just after you'd gone."

"So that's how you discover my secrets."

"I intend to find out all your secrets, darling. I intend to break down every barrier between us."

"You don't say." Sharisse was enjoying the light flirtation.

"But I just did, darling, and I'll be glad to tickle your ears with compliments all morning. Tell me where you're bound?"

"I'm for Winchley Manor to see Lady Winchley." She offered no further explanation. After all, how could she say that she was looking for an alternative transportation and company to London?

"I'll accompany you to their gates and then I'll wait and escort you back. I want to watch your style taking that last hedge on the way home. If something should go amiss, I'll be there to pick up the pieces."

She set her heels into her horse's sides and urged her into a canter. "You'll have a long wait for that, my lord." She was certain of both herself and her mount. She knew she ought to offer to introduce him to Belinda, but she didn't want him to hear what she had to say. It put her in a quandary, but since he had offered to wait, she'd just accept the offer at face value.

When she left Andrew dismounting in the adjacent field, she felt a twinge of remorse but put it behind her. She had more important matters to worry over.

She rode into Winchley with confidence that Belinda would see her no matter what she was engaged in. As a stableboy ran up to take her reins, she jumped down and strode to the side door. She pulled the bell.

Priscilla, Belinda's seventeen-year-old stepdaughter answered immediately.

"Sharisse! Come in and have a seat. It's a pleasure to see you. Did you come to visit with Mama?" She led the way to a small morning room. A light hint of rose-water perfume lingered behind the girl as she almost floated down the hall.

Sharisse noted how gracefully the girl moved. "Yes, I have a favor to ask of her. You are looking extremely well, Priscilla. Are you making plans in earnest yet for your season?"

Priscilla chatted easily about the arrangements that had been made for her benefit as they entered the cozy room. "Make yourself at home. I'll let her know you're here and send in a tea tray."

Instead of sitting, Sharisse walked about the room, her mind now concentrating on her problem. She would have liked to be able to confide the complete tale of her woes to Belinda, but she couldn't. If no one knew, then no one could inadvertently let anything slip. Sidney's death would remain a secret, but she could relate her fears about Andrew and enlist Belinda's help. Belinda had married an older man with an almost grown child and seemed to be able to handle the situation famously.

A servant brought in the tea tray with an assortment of biscuits and cucumber sandwiches. Belinda sailed into the room behind him, holding a kerchief to a reddened nose and watery eyes.

"Sharisse, my darling, you mustn't come near me. I think I'm coming down with a putrid sore throat. Dr. Bench says I must rest and drink lots of fluids. He left some horrid kind of powders for me to take." She took a chair on the opposite side of the room.

"I'm so sorry. I wouldn't have bothered you if I'd known. It's really the veriest nothing. I was planning a trip to London and thought you might like to accompany me. I was certain that you might like to have a trip to the muslin warehouse or to any of a number of shops with Priscilla's coming out soon."

"When I get over this sore throat, we certainly have our work cut out for us. Did you have some pressing business in London?"

Both women accepted a cup of tea from Priscilla.

"It's just that I need to see our solicitor. Sidney sent us a surprise in the arrival of his wife and mama-in-law, and I need to know how to go on." With Priscilla in the room, it would be impossible to confide in her friend.

Belinda set the cup down with a clink. "Sidney! Married and didn't tell you? I find it hard to believe. Did the girl have some proof?"

"I'm ashamed to admit that was my first thought, but her mama had a copy of their marriage lines and I recognized Sidney's signature. Why he didn't write me, I can't say. You'll have heard that he was seriously injured in India and they've sent him to Paris for special treatment. I don't know when we shall see him." Her voice broke on the last word and she shook herself to gain control.

Priscilla, a warmhearted girl, sank down beside Sharisse and put her arms around her. "You know, we'll do all we can to help you."

Belinda's eyes narrowed thoughtfully. "What is the bride like?"

That brought a smile. "She's a darling and could be just right for Sidney, but she has a dragon of a mother. The woman acts so vulgar, it's difficult to believe that she comes from a good family. She is attempting to take complete charge of the Meadows. I must find out where I stand."

"Oh, my dear, I'd love to go with you and support you, but I just can't make it." Belinda dabbed generously at her eyes.

Sharisse smiled. "I'll contrive. I always do, and when I return, I'll give you any news." She sat through a short discussion of Priscilla's season and then took her leave.

In moments she was back in the saddle, turning her mare toward the Meadows. Her head drooped with dejection and she sighed deeply. She wasn't quite certain when Andrew joined her, but his voice brought her up short.

"Can I help?" The voice was gravelly with emotion.

Sharisse had the almost overwhelming desire to lay the entirety of her problems on those broad shoulders and let him confront the worst, but she held back. There was too much at stake to risk heart, hand, and both her and Polly's future on such a course. She pasted her brightest smile on her face and called, "There is no need." With that she dug her heels into the horse's flanks. "Race you!" Her voice trailed back to him.

A muscle jumped in his cheek and he swore under his breath. The wind wore at his face as he urged his mount to greater speed, trying to catch up to his vixen. She would try the patience of a saint, and, Heaven help him, he was no saint. When would she learn to trust him? What could he do to encourage her? Was ever there such a coil?

CHAPTER NINE

Sharisse informed Mrs. Moffat of her journey as the coach stood at the door.

"Margaret might need the coach. How dare you take it without asking?" The woman's face was mottled with anger.

"Mama," interjected Margaret softly, "I'm not ready to go about the country yet. Sharisse, I hope you have a good trip. If you happen to go near the fabric warehouses, I'd like some flannel to make baby things."

"Margaret, I'd be happy to see to your needs." She turned to the older woman and murmured a stiff, "Good day."

She had no sooner closed the door on the coach when Andrew swept up the drive in his curricle. He stopped with a flourish next to her and eyed her with disapproval. "I see you're planning a trip. To London?"

"Yes. I should be back before dark, as I've only a couple of stops to make."

"I'm disappointed I'm not to have the pleasure of escorting you. I think you should have some protection, as there's no saying who you might meet on the road. I was about to offer to take you for a turn about the countryside, and ask your indulgence so you could show me our neighbors, but we can do that another day."

"Lord Brookfield," she began at her most formal, "you know that it's not possible for us to go to London under your protection."

He thought about that for a moment. In his day it had been very much the policy to escort ladies to their destination. Had times changed so much since he'd been gone? He decided to let the incident pass. He had no intention of arguing with her.

"I'll be available tomorrow for a turn about the countryside in your curricle, if you'd care to repeat your offer. Thank you for your concern. Have a nice day." She gave Timothy coachman the office to start and tied the strings of her flowered bonnet securely under her chin. With that she sat back and relaxed.

Polly began to chatter about her projected treat to the zoo while her maid listened eagerly, her face wreathed in smiles. The coach swayed easily on its leather hinges and bumped occasionally as the wheels encountered ruts, but the girls were far too distracted to notice.

Sharisse closed her eyes and contemplated the well-muscled figure she'd left behind. Andrew held a special attraction for her. Was it a forbidden attraction? No, she'd stake her life on the fact that he was an honorable man. If that were so, then there was no possibility that he was presently married. She'd set the solicitor on the trail. That would give the dear man something other than Sidney to think about. Yes, that might be the best course of action. What was it that Sidney maintained about trouble? "The best defense is a good offense." That was it. In this case, it just might answer. A broad smile curved her lips and she turned to view the countryside placidly, now that she had a campaign strategy.

It didn't take Lord Brookfield long to make a decision as he watched the retreating coach. He swung his horses around and set them to a slow pace following the coach.

"Sharisse, my darling, you're going to have a bit of protection whether you will it or not. All the trump cards will definitely not be in your hand. I always hold a few back for emergencies." He threw back his head and laughed. The day was going to prove quite interesting.

"Miss Sharisse, this be Lincoln's Inn Fields. Do ye want that I should pick ye up 'ere?"

Sharisse stepped out of the coach and shook her skirts into place. "Timothy, Polly and Dora are to have just one hour at the zoo. Then bring them back to me here." She admonished her charges, "Now remember, Polly, you are to stay with Dora. Under no circumstances are you to wander away from her. Dora, I'm holding you responsible for Polly. Be on your best behavior, both of you." She pulled a pound note from her reticule and handed it to Polly. "This is more than you'll need but it will allow the two of you to have some toffee or whatever treat you'd like."

Polly carefully tucked the note into her small reticule, a miniature replica of her sister's. "We promise, Sharisse. We'll do just as we ought."

Sharisse waved them good-bye and, seeing the brass plate proclaiming CRITCHFIELD AND CRITCHFIELD, SOLICITORS, took a deep breath to gather herself and opened the door. She had some misgivings about leaving the girls, but surely at the zoo they couldn't get into trouble.

The room she entered was large but somber. She decided that it reflected the attitude of its occupants. A young man was seated behind a desk, quill in hand, poring over a ledger. He looked up as he heard the door and, seeing Sharisse, rose to greet her.

"May I be of service, miss?" He rubbed his hands self-consciously on his pants before offering one to her.

"I have no appointment, but if Mr. Critchfield, Senior, is in, I believe that he'll see me. Tell him Miss Satterleigh is here."

"Very good, Miss Satterleigh. Won't you have a seat? I'll be right back."

Within moments she was ushered into the old gentleman's office.

"My dear Miss Satterleigh, this is a pleasant surprise." He took her hand in his and pressed it gently.

Sharisse gave a trill of laughter. "And when did I become Miss Satterleigh? I'm far more accustomed to Rissy."

The faded gray eyes smiled lovingly at her. "Now you're such a fine young lady I thought I owed you a bit more formality."

"Dear Uncle Ned, you should know me better than that.

Does this mean I have to call you Mr. Critchfield?" she inquired saucily.

"My dear, your father and I were best of friends all our lives and I was highly complimented to be given the honorary title of uncle. I'm not about to give it up now."

His welcome was so warm and kind, it was all Sharisse could do to keep from crying. She needed a sympathetic person she could count on, and this man was closer to a father than anyone else left on the face of the earth, but she knew him to be such a stickler for treading the straight path that she dared not confide the whole of her problem.

She sat down in a tall straight chair whose seat was highly polished from years of service. It was obvious that Mr. Critchfield didn't believe in spending his money on unnecessary luxuries. He was what was known as a warm man. He could make his money go twice as far as the next man. She loosened the strings of her bonnet, removing it and holding it on her lap. Summoning up her courage, she began her campaign with, "I'm in trouble."

When she saw the fire leap into the old man's eyes, she quickly returned, "No, no, you misunderstand. As you will recall, before Sidney left for India, he had you draw up some legal documents that put me in charge of the Meadows, in case of Papa's death, while he was gone."

Critchfield sat back in his chair and listened intently after ringing a brass bell twice. His fingers were pressed together and he alternately pushed and relaxed them unconsciously. "I've rung for tea. You've had a long journey, and it might help you to relax."

Sharisse smiled, knowing the dear soul was doing his best to put her at her ease and to keep from barking questions at her. She wondered when the whole of the truth came out, if he would ever forgive her for not letting him in on the tale in its entirety.

Sharisse took her courage in her hands. "Have you heard from Sidney?"

"As a matter of fact I have."

A lump hardened in Sharisse's stomach and she found it difficult to draw a breath while she waited for him to go on.

"Sidney wrote and enclosed a copy of a wedding certificate and made a will in favor of his wife, giving her an easy competence. Surely you received one at the same time? This came on last month's ship."

Sharisse's lips compressed so firmly together that the complete lower portion of her face turned white. "I'll kill him myself. He never wrote a word."

"Sharisse!"

She ignored his shocked protest. "Do you know what has happened? I have had his wife, in expectation of a *petit paquet*, and his mama-in-law descend upon us at the Meadows without a moment's notice. The situation has become totally intolerable." She jumped up from her chair and paced the floor steadily.

After a short knock on the door, the young man from the front desk brought in a tea tray, smiled shyly, bowed, and withdrew.

Critchfield didn't comment until he had poured her a steaming hot cup and offered it to her. "I understand, my dear."

"It's not that I don't want to welcome Sidney's wife. She's a pretty, complaisant little thing, just the kind of girl to suit Sidney. It's her mother! The woman is terrifying the servants, threatening to dismiss the lot of them, and riding roughshod over Polly at the same time. Naturally, the servants are not used to this kind of treatment and have banded together against her. Polly has even played some of her pranks on the woman to try to even the score."

Critchfield sipped his tea, his eyes narrowing thoughtfully. "And how does this lady treat you?" he asked mildly.

"As though I were a nuisance that could be removed at any time." She put down her cup, clasping her hands to give her courage. "The big problem is that we did receive a letter on this last ship. It came from the Commissioner at Delhi. It said" —here she took a deep breath, set her jaw, and plunged forward—"that Sidney was seriously injured and has been sent to a hospital in France. It sounded as if they didn't expect him to recover." There—the tale was out.

Critchfield took off his glasses and industriously polished them on a snowy white kerchief while he gathered his thoughts. "You want to know what your position at the Meadows is now, and what it will be if Sidney doesn't come home."

He stated the case so matter-of-factly that Sharisse was amazed. "If Sidney should die, did he or Papa make any provision for me? I know you read Papa's will, but at the time, I wasn't attending too well." She picked up her cup and sipped while she waited for an answer.

"You must know your papa had no idea his time would come so soon. He was in excellent health and in the prime of his life. He had talked to me just before the accident, saying that he'd realized he hadn't made adequate provision for you in case of his demise but that he knew Sidney would see you'd never want." He pushed his cup on one side and appeared to be in deep thought.

She held her breath to see what further information he had to impart.

"Until Sidney returns or I hear of his demise, you are unquestionably in charge at the Meadows. You handle all the servants, business, moneys, etc., and no accounting is to be made of it when such arrangements are terminated. You will always have your dress allowance, which is only a pittance if you chose to live on it, but in the event you marry, a very large settlement is yours." The intelligent old eyes seemed to pierce her.

"I have a rather delicate question to ask you, then. Andrew Lindley has recently returned from India and come into the title Lord Brookfield. You may know that his father passed away last year." She grimaced and swallowed convulsively, taking several deep breaths before she was able to go on. "I want you to find out if he is married or if he ever was. Can you do that for me?"

"My dear, consider it done." The old eyes sparkled. "So

you've found someone that interests you? Hmmm, I seem to recall that he was a young hellion in his salad days. I would suspect that he's improved greatly with age. A reformed rake might just suit you, my dear."

Sharisse was uncomfortable under the thoughtful stare. "Can I open Satterleigh House? Perhaps if I were away from the Meadows for a time, the new Lady Satterleigh and her mama could settle down."

"It think it an excellent idea. Feel free to call upon the estate for *any*," he particularly stressed the word *any*, "moneys that you might need to open the town house. If you find you need any more assistance, please call upon me. No matter what kind of coil you find yourself in, remember I'm here to give you a hand."

The warmth and kind understanding in the old man's voice was almost her undoing, but she merely gulped her tears and gave him a watery smile. Knowingly or not, he'd answered her problems. She could draw a large sum of money from the bank to tide them over until she could find a suitable husband and Mr. Critchfield would not ask for an accounting of the funds. She just needed to accomplish it before Sidney's death became known—in fact, the sooner the better. She would start the removal to Satterleigh House immediately.

Polly and Dora were wriggling in excitement. Neither girl had been to the zoo before and were eagerly anticipating its delights. In a short time Timothy coachman pulled up in front of an imposing gate. There was a plate announcing the hours the zoo was open and underneath a smaller sign giving the price of entrance. The girls jumped out of the coach, Polly fishing in her reticule for the pound note. They hardly heard Timothy adjuring them to be ready in precisely one hour. He was off to the nearest inn to rest the horses and find some refreshment.

Dora held Polly's hand tightly as they looked about them in awe. Polly gave the attendant her money and watched as her change was counted out. They were waved through the gate to a line of cages. Somewhere ahead they could hear the roar of a lion and the scream of an elephant. Both girls shivered in pleased anticipation.

Andrew held his horses in with a firm hand as he followed Sharisse's coach through the crowded streets. He contemplated her change in attitude to him seemingly overnight. He ran over the events of the past few days and couldn't come upon a suitable excuse or reason. "Ahhh, the truth will out," he murmured as he watched Sharisse jump down from the coach and walk into the solicitor's establishment.

He began to wonder if Polly had something to do with her reversal in attitude. Could it be that because Polly had a temporary aversion to him, Sharisse would send him away? The thought seemed more than likely. Well then, it behooved him to bring Polly around post haste. He'd never had a problem dealing with children while he was in India. Somehow they'd gravitated to him naturally and he'd enjoyed them. Polly would be no exception. He decreed it. The little girl had shown him a bit more respect since he'd dusted her little derrière, but he had a feeling she hadn't forgiven him for it yet.

The traffic became heavier and he had to mind his team more carefully on the cobbled streets. He wondered where Timothy coachman was taking Polly and Dora, knowing that Sharisse would be tied up in the solicitor's office for some time to come.

He pulled up to a youth lounging outside the solicitor's building. "Here! he called to the lad.

"Ya want me, guv'nor?" He seemed anxious to please.

"Yes, I've a shilling for you if you can tell me if you heard where that carriage that just stopped here is going."

The boy straightened at the promise of such largess. "I 'eard little miss say sumpin' about ta zoo." He stretched out his grubby hand for the coin and clutched it tightly. He nodded quickly and took off at a dead run, as if he were afraid it might be recalled.

Lord Brookfield smiled benevolently. Where else indeed would a young child like to go while she waited for her sister? If he were any judge, Sharisse wouldn't want Polly to hear all she had to say and if his instinct was right, the child knew too much as it was. She could easily give Sharisse's secret away.

Knowing where he was bound made the trip a deal easier. He wound his way dexterously through the city traffic and wandering vendors. The constant clack and bump of carriage wheels on the cobbles, calls of vendors extolling their wares, and children banging sticks on fence pickets blended together to make cacophony of sound.

He reached the entrance just in time to see the Satterleigh coach drive off. He couldn't leave his team unattended, and he knew that they needed water and a rest before making the return drive. Timothy must have the same objective in mind and Lord Brookfield trusted him to find the nearest inn.

Soon a weatherbeaten sign appeared proclaiming the establishment to be the Cork and Bottle. The place was run down, but he was pleasantly surprised to find a postboy come running to take his horses.

"I won't be here long, but I'd like my cattle rubbed down and given a little water—not too much, mind." He jumped down and watched the boy lead the horses to the rear. He walked into the establishment, the room filled with smoke and reeking of strong spirits. A large number of patrons were all trying to talk above the din. It was clear the inn catered mostly to tradespeople.

He stood for a moment surveying the room, an imposing figure in his molded buckskins and shining topboots. Spotting Timothy, he walked over and greeted the man. "Good day."

The coachman stood so suddenly that he almost upset his tankard of ale. "Land sakes, me lord, but ye startled me." He threw Lord Brookfield a puzzled look. " 'Ow comes ye are in 'ere?"

"I happened to see you drop Miss Polly and another young girl at the zoo. I wonder that you can trust them not to get into mischief."

"I ain't got no call to say what young miss ken or ken't do," Timothy returned apologetically.

At the moment the host, wiping up the bar with a dirty rag, inquired what he'd have.

"I'll have a tankard of your home-brewed and if you have a bit of bread and cheese, it would suit me fine. Make it enough for two." He turned to the coachman. "You'll join me?"

Timothy moved with Lord Brookfield to an empty table and sat heavily in an old wooden chair. "Thank 'ee, me lord." After taking a healthy swig of his ale, he addressed the issue. "I admit I've been a bit uneasy in ma 'ead about leaving them even if it's only fer an 'our. Miss Polly, she's a rare one, up to all the nines. Not, mind ye, that she's a mean bone in 'er body, but she loves a bit of fun."

When he had drained the tankard, Lord Brookfield raised his hand to order a refill. When the host's wife arrived, the old man feasted his eyes greedily on the large repast she set in front of them. The woman was all compliance.

"It don't seem 'ardly right, me a eating with the likes of ye." Nevertheless, he reached hungrily for a slice of roast beef.

"Timothy, you're a man, same as I, and do your job to the best of your ability. Just because I've been born with a silver spoon in my mouth doesn't make me the better man."

"Oh, me lord," Timothy whispered urgently, "you'll 'ave the constable picking ye up iffen you're not careful." His eyes darted about to see who might have heard.

Andrew leaned over the table. "Timothy, I've worked with all kinds of men in my life and I think I've learned a thing or two about people. You, just like me, would defend the Crown with your last breath if need be. That gives us a common bond. I'm going to go escort the girls for the rest of their promenade about the zoo. There's plenty of time for you to finish the rest of the meal, but I have a strong urge to see just what Polly's up to." He took out his watch. "I'll deliver the girls to you at the front gate in half an hour."

"I'll be there, me lord."

Lord Brookfield stood up and the host rushed over. "Was everything to your satisfaction?"

"Please convey a message to your wife, that everything was prime." He handed the man a liberal donation and donned his top hat.

Outside he hailed a hackney.

"Where to, guv'nor?" the man inquired.

"The zoo," Lord Brookfield replied.

The hackney turned around with tilted head. "What's that?" The ways of the quality were clearly beyond him.

Andrew's eyebrow raised sardonically and he stared quizzically at the man.

"Beg pardon, guv'nor. The zoo it is."

The jarvey pulled up at the entrance and Lord Brookfield tossed him a coin that made the old man's eyes light up. "Thank ye kindly."

Andrew paid the fee and inspected the layout. Deciding which course the girls had probably taken, he set out to run the route in reverse. He hadn't gotten too far when he spotted them across the park near the monkey cage. Polly seemed to be having an animated conversation with some tough. The other girl was cowering behind Polly.

A muscle jerked in Lord Brookfield's neck and he strode purposefully across the midway. As he came within about fifty feet, he heard Polly cry, "I will not!" and see her draw one foot back and kick the man hard in the shin. When he doubled over to nurse the hurt, she stomped on his good foot and raised her fists. By that time, Andrew had closed the distance and when the man raised a hand to slap her, Andrew caught it, spun the tough around and planted a flush hit on the assailant's jaw and watched with grim satisfaction as the man stretched his length in the dirt.

He held out an arm to each girl. "Shall we go?"

Neither seemed disposed to stay and took quick advantage of the proffered arm.

"Have you seen all the attractions or may we make our way to the front gate?"

"Could we see the monkey house first? That man interrupted us before we had a chance to visit it." Polly turned soulful eyes to her benefactor.

"What did that man want, Polly?"

"He ordered me to give him my watch pin that my papa gave me and I told him I didn't have to." Her chin was set at a defiant angle.

"You did extremely well. There's just one more thing you need to know in case you are ever in a like situation. After you kicked the blackguard, you should have run like the devil toward the nearest crowd for protection."

"Are you going to scold me and tell Sharisse?" Polly inquired pertly. Dora's head hung in shame.

"Is that the kind of opinion you have of me?" He put a hand to his brow in a theatrical gesture. "I am undone!"

Polly giggled delightedly. "I still don't know how you found us."

"It's a rather involved story. Let me just say I had urgent business in London today and that I happened to be passing when you entered the zoo. Now tell me, who is your companion?"

"You don't know Dora? She's Sharisse's maid." Dora nodded proudly.

"Don't gammon me. Dora can't be old enough to be Sharisse's maid. I daresay she's not above fifteen."

"Hannah took sick day before yesterday and she sent her niece to help out until she is better. Sharisse says Dora might as well start training now."

They had viewed their fill of the monkeys when Lord Brookfield took out his watch. "I think that it's time for Timothy coachman to arrive."

The girls agreed, and he escorted them to the street to look for the coachman. Before long the coach lumbered into view. As he assisted Polly into the coach, Lord Brookfield murmured in a low voice, "Let's not worry Sharisse. Let's keep this our secret. Can you keep Dora quiet?"

A huge grin split Polly's cherubic face. "Without a doubt."

Andrew saluted them as they drove off.

Polly whispered conspiratorily to Dora, "Remember, this is a secret. You would be severely reprimanded, possibly even dismissed, if this escapade got back to the Meadows. You know, I'm beginning to think that Lord Brookfield isn't such a bad sort after all."

CHAPTER TEN

Sharisse pulled off her bonnet and gloves after she stepped out of the coach and stretched. It had been a tiring journey, but well worth the effort. She could breathe more easily now that she knew she was still in charge and she had the option of escaping to London at any time. She reflected that the time would be soon, as soon as she could make it.

Simms opened the door promptly. "We're glad to see you home, Miss Sharisse." The heartfelt tones would have wrung tears from someone far more hardened than she. "You know, Miss Sharisse, I'll go. I've told you many a time that when I can't do my work . . ."

Sharisse put a hand on Simms's shoulder. "Enough! I'll see that everything's made right before the night is over. I hope that you know how much I value your services. Trust me, I'll work it out." She forced a bright smile and ran lightly up the stairs to freshen up a bit before tackling the dragon.

Polly and Dora followed more leisurely. Polly's first stop was the kitchen. It had been a long ride and she felt in urgent need of some kind of sustenance. Cook always had a biscuit and a pastry ready for her.

She opened the door cautiously, peering into the large room before entering.

Françoise was in a tirade. *"Sacre nom de chien!* Something must be done about that woman. All day she's run roughshod over all of us and she don't know *chateaubriand* from *poulet.* Just wait till Mr. Sidney gets home. He'll straighten out things in a hurry. It's too bad Miss Sharisse is just too nice to set her down a peg."

Polly closed the door softly, her face screwed up in thought.

Sidney was not here and was not going to be, but she was here and she could do what Sharisse could not. She bit her thumb while ideas simmered in her fertile mind. Finally, her face cleared and a look that Sharisse would have recognized at a glance crossed her face. She headed for the side door and the garden.

Kneeling among the snapdragons, she started to search, paying no attention to the fact that she was kneeling in her good dress. Finally she spotted her other pet and, picking it up, carefully dropped it in her little reticule. Straightening up, she brushed herself off, giving a rueful stare at the dirt staining her sprig muslin. It didn't matter, for this was war. She headed back into the house and raced up the staircase. Mrs. Moffat's bedchamber was at the end of the hall and she knocked lightly.

Since there was no answer, she peered in cautiously. Mrs. Moffat was apparently gone. Polly reached into her reticule, pulled her pet from it, and placed it in the center of the large bed. The warmth of the spread must have appealed for it moved in a slow circle and settled down.

Polly had just closed the door behind her when Mrs. Moffat appeared in the hall.

"What are you doing by my bedchamber?" the woman thundered.

"See for yourself," Polly snipped, and raced down the hall to her room.

Mrs. Moffat entered the room cautiously, not seeing anything disturbed. She began to relax. When she moved over to the dressing table to rearrange her coiffure, she turned to throw her shawl on the bed. That was when she saw the snake coiled by her pillow. She screamed in fright and then clamped her lips shut in fury. That was just what the child expected of her—to run from the place screaming.

"Well, Miss Polly Satterleigh, I've been threatening to teach you a lesson, and today is the day." She picked up the hairbrush and marched down the hall to Polly's room.

She tore the door open without benefit of a knock. Polly was staring out the window grinning, having heard the scream. She hadn't expected the woman to retaliate, and her face showed shock as she saw the hairbrush.

"Sharisse! Rissy! Help me!" Polly screamed the words.

"Save your breath. This time you're going to get what's coming to you, you little brat." She advanced into the room.

Polly darted about to and fro, keeping a piece of heavy furniture between her and the angry woman.

Sharisse heard Polly's voice as she came from her bedchamber. She knew in an instant what was wrong and she flew down the hall to Polly's room.

As she entered the open door, she saw Mrs. Moffat with a raised hairbrush and Polly cowering behind a chair. "Mrs. Moffat! What is the meaning of this?" Sharisse's voice held a great deal of suppressed anger, and her face clearly showed her displeasure.

"If you won't teach this child a lesson, I will. She put a snake on my bed." She turned a malevolent stare at Polly. "It's far past time that someone taught her some manners."

"Polly, go put Lovey out and then find Miss Roberts and have her help you dress for dinner. Mrs. Moffat, I'd like to speak with you in the blue salon in, let's say, ten minutes."

With that both girls were gone, leaving a speechless Mrs. Moffat to berate an empty room. Finding no one to hear her imprecations, she ceased and disgruntledly stomped downstairs to await Sharisse.

Sharisse took her time arriving, cooling her temper and planning her attack carefully. When she entered the blue salon she was met with a subdued guest.

"I regret that Polly scared you with her pet snake, but I believe that you have been guilty of trespassing the bounds of good manners, Mrs. Moffat, to have a little plain speaking. I have returned home to hear discord from every corner of the Meadows. I find that all the servants are threatening to leave if something isn't done about your breach of etiquette."

"If the servants all leave, this place will be far better for it. The entire lot of them aren't up to the standards that I've been used to. Margaret will want to make some big changes and additions to the staff and I intend to guide her choices."

"Mrs. Moffat, I don't believe that you quite understand the way things stand here. Sidney left me in complete charge of the Meadows, and until his return I will say what is to be done and no one else. If you prove not to be able to accept our hospitality graciously, I will take steps to remove you from the Meadows. I would not like to see Margaret separated from her mother when her lying-in time comes, but I will do whatever is necessary to keep the peace with my staff. Further, it is not your place to reprimand Polly. I will not tolerate your interference with her upbringing again. Let me assure you that Lady Margaret will please Sidney when the time comes, and your advice will fall on deaf ears. I suggest strongly that you reconsider your position here and make do."

She closed the salon door behind her and left Mrs. Moffat to make what she would of the situation. Congratulating herself on her handling of the unwanted task, she moved on to the next phase. "Simms?" she called heading toward the butler's pantry.

"Yes, miss?" The old butler stuck his head out the door, a piece of silver and polish cloth still in his hand.

"I am going to open Satterleigh House and I want you to oversee the details. Jenkins can remove to the country for a breath of fresh air while you organize the staff."

A watery smile and a nod answered her. The old man was far too choked with emotion to speak.

Then Sharisse stepped lightly up the stairs to see Margaret. Nurse was patiently teaching her to hold a pair of knitting needles and make the proper movements.

Margaret looked up and smiled charmingly. "Sharisse, see what I am learning? Nurse is so helpful."

Sharisse took a chair opposite. "I just wanted to talk to you for a moment. Margaret, how would you feel about staying here at the Meadows in charge of the estate while I go up to London for a few weeks?"

Margaret's look of dismay told Sharisse how the girl felt, and she set about trying to reassure her.

"I find it necessary to spend some time in London, but I'm not that far away that I can't get back within a very short time if you find that you need me. I assure you I don't mean to desert you. When your time comes for lying in, I promise you I'll be here to support you. Besides, nurse will stay with you as will all the servants except Simms. I find that I'll need him in London. Mrs. Brown, our housekeeper, will spend some time each day teaching you all you'll need to know about running the house, and the bailiff will take care of all business matters."

Sharisse waited to see how Margaret reacted before going on. "You must remember that the servants will answer only to you, so you might suggest to your mama that she refrain from changing your orders. I have spoken to her at length on the subject and believe that she will now let you receive the respect and courtesy you are due. Remember that each of the servants holds a special place in Sidney's heart and that he would be gravely displeased if one were to leave for any reason."

Margaret looked bewildered. "Sharisse, Mama doesn't realize . . . Perhaps she . . . I feel quite badly that she has upset the household so. I hope I know my duty to my mama, but now that I'm a married lady I can't help but feel my duty to my husband comes first. Oh, Sharisse, he is the most wonderful gentleman."

It was Sharisse's turn to feel the prickle of tears. How well she knew her brother. He could get into all sorts of predicaments, but he had always managed to pull himself out despite the odds. It was a standard joke between them. Sidney was like a cat—he had several lives. She pulled herself together. "You can always send one of the stableboys up to London to get me if you have need. Meantime, you can work on getting together the baby clothes you'll need. One of the footmen will be bringing up the package I picked up for you at the warehouse."

"Thank you. That was kind, Sharisse. I wish that you didn't have to go. I feel that Mama is driving you away."

"Don't. I want to spend some time in London and you'll find that you'll adjust more easily if I'm not available. If you have any question as to what to do in any situation, just ask yourself what Sidney would do or if he would like it and judge your actions accordingly." With that, Sharisse took her leave.

Having come this far, she decided to interview the staff and tell them of her decision. There were many details to attend to and she could see she'd be busy for the next few days getting ready to make the move.

The first problem on her plate was that of a chaperone. She didn't have any suitable relatives to invite to stay and she knew the *ton* would look down their noses if she arrived without one. Then it struck her. Adelaide Roberts had been with the family serving as a governess and companion for years. Although the woman had come into a sum of money several years back, she wouldn't consider leaving Sharisse. It was quite true that Miss Roberts was eccentric, but then Sharisse had heard that eccentrics were the latest rage in town. Miss Roberts was just the thing to add respectability to her household.

She would see that all three of them had several new gowns before they left and many more when they arrived in town, and no one need know that they had been living in a retired manner at the Meadows.

CHAPTER ELEVEN

Sharisse had finished her breakfast, informed the staff of her decision, and was mentally making a list of things to be accomplished before she could remove to London, when she became aware that Andrew was standing at her elbow.

"Now, my love, out with it. What is it that's bothering you? I'm just the man to take care of all your problems if you'll only share them." He raised her hand to his lips and kissed it lightly. "You are all I desire on the face of this earth."

His eyes held hers and she felt a strange burning sensation that caused her knees to feel weak. "I wish you wouldn't say things like that."

"Why not? It happens to be true and it throws you into such a delightful flutter." His smile was warm. "You blush charmingly, you know," he added conversationally.

To Sharisse it was like a dash of cold water on her heating passions. It was much safer to be annoyed with the man.

"I have much on my mind just now. I've decided that the air in London at this season would be beneficial for Polly's health and I would enjoy a slight respite from the arduous duties of the Meadows."

"Just so. I don't know how you tolerate that dragon of a woman at all." His voice was suitably grave but his eyes were laughing. "Are you leaving the servants here?"

"All but Simms and Miss Roberts. The air in London will do Simms a deal of good too."

Andrew caught the inflection easily. "And Miss Roberts, does she suffer from the same malady?" His eyes crinkled with laughter.

Sharisse allowed herself to smile. "No, I believe that she is above such petty things. Her *ton* is much loftier than mine. She doesn't take offense easily."

"I'm concerned for you being in London alone. It's hardly the place for a young girl."

Sharisse gave a trilling laugh. "Polly and I will hardly be alone with a retinue of servants. I'll add to the staff as I see the need. Moreover, I'm really of the age I should start wearing caps."

"Don't gammon me, darling. If I see you wearing one of those ridiculous wisps of lace the old matrons seem to think necessary, I'll take steps to remove it."

"Now that would set all the old tabbies' tongues to wagging." Their lighthearted banter was a pleasant interchange after the events of last evening and her confrontation with Mrs. Moffat.

"I've already done that. I'll have to return to Lindley House in London and see what the *ton* makes of me these days. Would you like to make a wager that I'll find myself popular?" He raised a quizzical eyebrow at her.

"You're outrageous. However, if you do get up to London, be sure to visit me. I promise not to turn you away."

"Are you certain that Polly can be trusted to behave herself in London?"

"I plan to add a suitable footman to accompany Polly and her maid, just for safety's sake."

"That's a fine idea, one that I might have suggested myself."

Sharisse studied him skeptically and asked thoughtfully, "Now what do you know about Polly that I seem to have missed?"

"It's just that she has a propensity for inventing mischief. Trouble seems to be her middle name."

His eyes caressed her and she felt herself growing warm under his appraisal. Her breathing seemed to be difficult to catch and her pulse became erratic. She should fly from this flame, but just like the moth, she couldn't.

"It certainly is," she agreed with a touch of asperity. I'm

hoping that removing to London will have a beneficial effect on her manners."

He laughed outright. "It might at that. I hope it has a beneficial effect on you too. I'd like to see a deal more of you."

Sharisse smiled and tossed back, "In London, I must abide strictly by the rules, so you'd have to declare your intentions before I could allow you any more license than what you already have."

It didn't take long to settle into Satterleigh House. An unenthusiastic Jenkins accepted his sojourn into the country with equinimity. Simms was delighted with the change and was busily interviewing applicants for the various positions.

Sharisse was sitting in the small morning room when Simms approached.

"If you please, Miss Sharisse, I have an applicant at the door for a position of footman." He drew himself up in such a way that she knew exactly how he felt about the man. "He has some unusual recommendations. I thought it best if you would see him."

Sharisse was puzzled. If anyone knew his duty, it was Simms, and if the would-be footman didn't measure up, Simms would be the first one to send him packing. Her curiosity was aroused and she rose to follow the butler.

She looked over the candidate critically, noting his mammoth size. He wasn't the least bit like what she thought a footman ought to look like. This man had unusually broad shoulders and long, powerful arms. He was approaching middle age and his nose had a decided list to one side as if it had been broken at some time. His face bordered on the ugly except when he smiled, which he did upon seeing Sharisse.

"Good morning. Your name is . . . ?" she inquired politely.

"Flynn, ma'am. I'd like to work for you. Lord Brookfield suggested ye'd need some more 'elp and that 'e'd go bail fer me."

That brought a chuckle. She had said she was going to look

for a suitable footman for Polly, and Andrew had sent her this man.

"And how long have you known Lord Brookfield?"

"I knew him afore 'e left fer foreign parts and then 'e looked me up when 'e come back."

He said it simply and Sharisse believed him. "You mean you've worked with him at Brookfield Hall?"

"No, ma'am. 'E stopped in where I was aworkin' and asked me ta come over ta ye."

"Are you saying that Lord Brookfield is now in London?"

"Yessum. 'E's opened Lindley 'Ouse and said ye'd need a good strong man ta keep the riffraff out."

Sharisse burst out laughing. "Flynn, do you by chance like children?"

"Yes, ma'am. We usually gets along fine."

The warmth of his smile told Sharisse that he was sincere. "Very well. I'll hire you on a probationary basis."

"Begging yer pardon, miss, but what does that mean?"

"It means that we'll try you out and see if your services prove acceptable."

"That'd be fine. Ye'll be safe in this 'ouse as long as I'm in it."

Simms signaled the man to follow him and left the room muttering something about ordering a livery in a gorilla size.

"Robbie," called Sharisse as she entered the crimson salon, "I find it necessary to go out to the silk warehouse and order materials for new gowns for both of us. I'll also stop in Bond Street and see if there's something already made up that I can use. I'm going to leave Polly with you, as I want to hurry."

"Go ahead and do your shopping, but I don't need anything." Miss Roberts dropped her knitting and stared at Sharisse. "I can well afford a few new gowns, but I don't particularly admire the new fashion plates we've been through."

"It's a necessity that you look extremely smart and I'm certain that with a little more looking I'll be able to find something to suit you quite well."

Miss Roberts made a clucking sound, shaking her head, and

finally, after Sharisse had begged her prettily, the old woman acquiesced.

Polly watched Sharisse and Hannah drive off from her bedchamber window. Deciding that it might be a good time to see what treats the London cook kept in her kitchen, she sauntered down the back stairs and surveyed the room.

"Well, missy, what can I do for you?" The cook looked intently at the little girl.

"If you please, I'm hungry. Have you got a few biscuits or a pastry or two?" She raised a cherubic face to the woman and managed to look as if she'd not had a bite to eat for three days.

Thus appealed to, the cook went over to a large jar and removed a few biscuits and set them out on a plate. Noting the condition of Polly's hands, she suggested mildly, "You wash up and straighten your pinafore and then you can have these."

If that was the price, Polly was perfectly willing to pay. She headed for the sink and proceeded to make generous use of the water and soap. Then she adjusted her dress, retied the sash, and took the comb out of the pocket of her pinafore and dusted her bangs. She turned to cook, "Now?"

The woman smiled benevolently.

She sat at the table and munched happily. When she was through she gave cook a gracious compliment on her fare and set the seal on a return performance. Polly ambled to the front parlor to see what the street had to offer in the way of entertainment, when she heard the knocker on the door.

Eager to see who their first visitors could be, she danced out into the hall to catch a peek. When she heard Simms announce that Miss Satterleigh was not at home, she went forward immediately.

"If you please, I couldn't help but hear you are calling on my sister. She should be back at any time and would hate to find she'd missed your call. Won't you come in and wait for a few minutes?" Polly was on her best behavior, her manners fit to please even the greatest sticklers. "My name is Elizabeth, but everyone calls me Polly." She smiled becomingly.

One lady looked at the other and then they nodded. Simms

stepped back to allow them passage and, though he gave Polly a sharp stare, he remained silent.

Polly winked at him and gave him her most brilliant smile. She led the ladies into the small drawing room, which had been thoroughly polished and was furnished with excellent taste. The ladies looked around and seemed to approve.

"I am Lady Jersey, and this is my friend Mrs. Burrell. We met your sister when she was presented a few years ago. We saw that she had cards to Almack's. She is a very lovely young lady and we were sorry when she left London to go back to the country."

Polly was only eleven, but she knew the names of all the patronesses of Almack's by heart and how important it was to be favored by them. She was filled with excitement at the opportunity that had been given her. Here was something she could do for Sharisse. Folding her hands primly in her lap, she introduced herself and expressed her delight in meeting them.

"How is Sidney faring in India?" inquired Lady Jersey politely.

"He was wounded and sent to France. It is one of the reasons that we came to London, so that if Sharisse gets word, she can go to him quickly." Here Polly took a deep breath and launched what she thought was her campaign to help Sharisse get a rich husband. "She wasn't overly excited about coming, since she's found out that father left her a great deal of money. She's afraid that she'll be the target of fortune hunters, but I know you ladies will help her find someone suitable."

She managed to speak so ingenuously that neither lady hesitated to believe her.

Mrs. Burrell, usually the more serious patron, laughed outright. "Sally, I've never been so delightfully approached." To Polly she added, "I will keep her in mind."

Conversation became general and after a few minutes the patronesses rose to take their leave.

"We're sorry to have missed your sister, but tell her we called and are looking forward to seeing her again."

As the ladies gave their coachman the signal to be off, Lady Jersey commented, "I don't know when I've been so entertained by a youngster. If Sharisse has overcome her shyness and portrays the vivacity Elizabeth does, I don't think that she'll need much help from us to find a suitable *parti.*"

Lord Brookfield rang the bell at Lindley House. The knocker was off the door, signifying that no one was in residence, but he had no doubts that Spencer would answer the door.

"Mr. Andrew! I never thought to see you." The old voice trembled, but the faded gray eyes warmed the second they saw him. The butler had a crop of snowy white hair and maintained a dignified posture even in his advancing years.

"It's good to be home again, Spencer. I trust you are well and plan to stay with me."

"Thank you, my lord. I would consider it an honor to serve yourself." He took Lord Brookfield's coat and hat. "We are short-staffed at the present, but if you like, I'll remedy that."

"Do that and, Spencer"—he looked intently at the butler—"increase everyone's wages as you see fit. I want the best of everything and expect to get it."

Spencer nodded, understanding his lordship as easily as he had in the old days. Lord Brookfield was letting him know that money wasn't going to be a problem and that he was offering top wages in order to get the best help.

"Tell cook to expect me for dinner at seven o'clock and see that these Holland covers are removed by the time I return. I know that I can count on you."

"That you can, my lord. I'll see to everything." The old man beamed his happiness.

Andrew climbed back into his curricle and gave his team the office to start. Behind him Spencer was calling for help to assist in unloading the coach, and a flurry of activity began.

Andrew whistled a light turn and nodded pleasantly to several members of the aristocracy as he tooled his cattle through the park, heading for Grosvenor Place. It was quite satisfying to be the object of much speculation. He well knew the adage, "Never admit to a fault." He intended to demand his rightful place with the *ton* and carve himself a niche that would insulate Sharisse against the spiteful biddies who were always about.

The butler at his aunt's greeted him affectionately and ushered him to his aunt's side.

"Well, Andrew, I see you've decided to come home, but let me tell you, if you've come to hang on me sleeve you're fair and far out."

It was a daunting welcome, but Andrew seemed to pay it no mind. He merely smiled and kissed the old woman in lavender satin. She wore a lace cap tied becomingly under her chin and her brown eyes scrutinized him carefully.

"Now, my dear aunt, have I ever applied to you for monetary relief? I'm calling on you as my only living relative. I wouldn't want to be backward in my attentions."

"When you start buttering up this old stick, I begin to think that you want something." Aunt Clarissa, known to the world as Lady Englethorpe, was shrewd and usually hit her target when she launched an arrow.

"As a matter of fact, there is something you might do for me if you have a mind to help me. Do you remember the Satterleighs? Sir Robert Satterleigh was on the town some years ago. He had three children, Sidney, Sharisse, and Elizabeth. I'd like to procure Sharisse a card to Almack's."

His aunt chortled. "I'd like to see you accomplish it."

"You know very well that it is impossible for a single male to do so. But you, with your influence could get an unknown country bumpkin a card if you so chose. Will you help me?"

"Just what is your relationship to this girl, Andrew?"

"My, what a commonplace mind you seem to have acquired, Aunt. Do you think that I'd set up one of my flirts with an entree to Almack's?" He leaned forward in his chair.

His aunt's eyes had danced as she made her accusation, knowing full well that there must be more to this tale than

Andrew was letting on. "Go on. Don't keep an old woman in suspense."

Andrew could see that she was clearly having a gay time. "I'll let you in on the secret, but I don't want it nosed abroad yet. I plan to make her my wife as soon as she's had time to enjoy the season. She hasn't any idea of my plans for her yet, so I'd appreciate your silence."

She permitted herself a dry chuckle. "And Sharisse—does she find you irresistible?"

"No. I'm not even positive that she likes me. She has recently gone out of her way to avoid me."

"You are going to relieve the boredom besetting me lately, Andrew. I can't remember when I've been so entertained. So, all you require of me is a card to Almack's? You're not in need of funds?"

"Yes, Aunt Clarissa, the card is all I stand in need of." His lips curved upward. "I believe that I can be quite comfortable with what I brought back from India with me. You know fifteen years is quite enough time to make one's fortune."

"And did you make your fortune?" she asked skeptically.

"Let's just say that I have more than enough to see to my needs, and once the matchmaking mamas get wind of it, I'll be the matrimonial prize of the season. If possible, I'd like to have my future with Sharisse settled by then."

"Money covers a multitude of sins. However, there are many who will remember your past indiscretions. I think it behooves me to see you reestablish your credit quickly, and one of the best ways is to marry suitably. Sharisse Satterleigh is of good family and I see no impediment to the union." Her laughter punctuated her conversation.

Andrew looked appropriately humble. "Thank you, Aunt Clarissa. I will appreciate your efforts upon my behalf, and if at any time I may return the favor, please feel free to call upon me."

"I just might do that, Andrew. You amuse me. I think that I might even join the social whirl this season, if only to see what a merry dance your young woman leads you on."

CHAPTER TWELVE

Sharisse was agreeably surprised at the number of morning callers who arrived in the next few days. She could forgive Polly for entertaining two of the patronesses of Almack's without her, for they had indeed sent her a voucher for the famous club. What puzzled her beyond all was the number of matrons she didn't know who called on the flimsiest excuses and disclosed the information that they had sons who were desirous of meeting her.

She received a large number of cards to routs, balls, and al fresco breakfasts. As Sharisse pondered which to accept, Simms announced, "Lord Brookfield."

She glanced up, a broad smile showing she was pleased to see him. With a flourish, she shook out her skirts and stood up, putting both hands out.

He took them, raising first one and then the other to his lips, and kissed them gently. After studying her daffodil morning gown of sprigged muslin, decorated with bits of ribbon and lace, and seeing her hair trussed up stylishly in a loose knot at the back with cascading curls falling from it, he raised an eyebrow. "I see you are quite enjoying London." Noting the stack of cards on the table, he added, "It seems you've become a social butterfly."

She laughed up at him. "Isn't it exciting? Poor Miss Roberts is going to be worn out if I drag her to all these parties."

"I'll be more than happy to escort you to any or all of them and can promise you that I'll see Miss Roberts tucked away in a corner where she might be comfortable." He took stock of her gown and smiled his approval.

"I believe that I'm of the age to dispense with a chaperon

but I don't want to hurt Miss Roberts's feelings." Sharisse eyed the gold coat that molded his superb frame with admiration. Cream-colored small clothes complete the toilette and his boots had a high shine.

"Rubbish! If you don't know your worth, let me tell you that I do. You'll be suitably escorted wherever you go and no nonsense about it."

"Pooh." Sharisse delighted in seeing his temper rise a bit. The man was far too complacent to suit her. What he needed was a good set down.

"It's plain to see that you need a firm hand on the reins and I'm just the man for the job."

"And, pray tell, who asked you to be my keeper?" Her foot tapped dangerously but she was reveling in the confrontation.

"I assumed the task of my own free will the day we met. I'm willing that you should enjoy yourself—God knows you deserve it—but when it's over, I expect to claim my own."

Sharisse digested his remarks in shocked silence. She had wanted to shake him up a bit, but she hadn't quite expected this. The man acted as though she were his fiancée, and the arrogant soul had never even broached the subject. As soon as Critchfield confirmed that he was single, she could consider the matter, but he was fair and far out if he thought he could ride roughshod over her.

Polly skipped into the room humming a lively tune. When she saw Lord Brookfield she greeted him cordially.

"I see my credit has risen, Polly. Are we friends yet?" His manner was teasing.

Polly thought about it for a minute. "I'm not certain, but I think we're making progress." She turned to her sister. "May I walk over to Green Park? It's not too far. Flynn tells me they're planning a balloon ascension and the balloonists are setting it up." Polly's expression would have melted an iceberg.

"You need some exercise and I don't see any reason you can't go. Be sure to take one of the footmen, Polly."

Andrew spoke up. "May I suggest that you send Flynn along

too. He loves a good walk and I guarantee she'll come to no harm with him along."

"You're a trump. Is that all right, Sharisse?" Polly danced about while waiting for the answer.

"Be off with you." Sharisse smiled fondly at her younger sister and waved her from the room. "Now, about Flynn. Tell me how you found him."

"I have my sources. You'll just have to trust me." His smile was quite warm and his eyes softened as he spoke.

"Why should I, my lord?" Her eyes bespoke their challenge.

He stepped closer and raised her chin. "Because you want to, darling. Listen to your heart and make room for me." His eyes bespoke his rising passion.

"You're asking much of me. What am I to receive in return?" she quizzed him breathlessly. Her legs felt as if they wouldn't support her much longer and her heart was hammering in her chest. It seemed to chant, "Trust him, trust him."

"Everything that you desire. Your wish is my command." He lowered his lips to hers and sealed her protest. His tongue tested and tasted the soft recesses of her mouth and he could feel her resistance wane.

Sharisse was hardly aware of their surroundings. Her attention was focused entirely on the virile figure enclosing her in his arms. A tingling sensation spread its warmth throughout her body and she thought she might collapse from the intensity. She was well aware that the situation was beyond her control; she also found that she did trust Andrew, utterly and completely. She heard a low moan and realized that it was coming from her throat. Abruptly she tore herself away from him and stared into his eyes, her bosom heaving and her face flushed.

He scrutinized her thoroughly, seeming to be quite satisfied with what he saw. "I won't take advantage of you, my darling, but I wish to share all you have to give me."

"Are you declaring your intentions, Andrew?" she inquired, trying to sound light and teasing. But she succeeded only in convincing him of her sincerity.

"What would you answer me if I were?" he responded with equal candor.

"I don't know." She was still waiting to hear from her solicitor on the matter. "I think that it is too soon to know."

"If that's the case, I'm glad I'm not declaring my intentions at the moment. I would hate to have you not know your mind if I were to put the question to the test." His eyes seemed to laugh, but his tone was serious.

Sharisse didn't quite know what to make of his comments. At first she thought he was serious and then she decided that she'd mistaken his meaning. While she was pondering the idea, he changed the subject and the prickling immediacy of the moment was gone.

"My Aunt Englethorpe will be calling upon you in the next day or two. She is planning a ball sometime in the next two weeks and would like your company. I will be glad to escort you and can promise the cream of society will be present."

"I'll give it consideration." She resolved that he shouldn't have everything his way.

"You'll do more than that, Sharisse. I have reason to believe that Prinny himself will be there. Aunt Englethorpe will command several dukes and some of the Members of Parliament. You can't afford to miss this opportunity."

"Well, I haven't yet received my invitation, so I'll just have to wait and see." Her eyes sparkled as she saw his brow crease.

"I'm counting upon you to relieve the boredom of the evening. Without you the ball will be decidedly flat." His polished address hit its mark and Sharisse conceded.

"Oh, all right. I'll come if it means that much to you." There was a question in her voice.

"Thank you, darling, and yes, it does mean a great deal to me." After making a few light remarks about some of the places she might like to visit, he kissed her once lightly.

"May I have the pleasure of your company on the morrow to take you riding in the park?" His manner was formal but his demeanor was intimate.

The ambiguity held her attention. "Yes, I'd enjoy that. What time would you like me to be ready?"

"Would eight o'clock be too early?"

"I would have you know I'm not town bred and we still arise with the sun. I can be ready quite easily by that hour."

After his departure, Sharisse made her way through the house to see that all was in place. When she entered the library she saw that Simms had put out several copies of the London *Gazette*. She picked up the oldest one first. Thumbing through it, she found the society page and noted that it stated Miss Sharisse Satterleigh, sister of Sir Sidney Satterleigh, was now in residence and could be found in Grosvenor Square. She wondered who had put the item in, but perhaps it explained why she had had so many callers in the last few days.

She scanned the rest of the latest gossip and mentally filed away the information, thinking that some of the *on dits* might be of use in her social whirl.

Closing the paper, she saw an amusing cartoon on the back page. It was a picture of the Regent standing with both pockets pulled out of his trousers, revealing them to be empty. The caption read, "Who is my friend today?" The caricature was delightful, depicting the man's perplexed face.

The mention of the Regent reminded Sharisse of Andrew's Aunt Englethorpe's ball. Andrew had been charmingly insistent that she attend. Just what was the man's interest? Was he going to declare his intentions or was he amusing himself at her expense? Somehow she couldn't bring herself to think of him as married. Was that just wishful thinking? No, Andrew was too much a gentleman and a man of his word. He wouldn't stoop so low. With a sigh she picked up the next copy to see what news she ought to know.

Polly was enjoying her walk in the park. With Flynn in attendance, she didn't worry a bit about being accosted. The new footman had no trouble keeping up with her quick pace and Polly was quite happy to view the balloon apparatus being set up.

There was a wicker basket that Polly assumed was what the men rode in and a metal thing that she heard someone say was the burner. The large balloon was stretched out in the grass and the balloonists were busy checking the rigging. Nothing seemed to be happening and after a few minutes of watching, Polly began to wander about.

She hadn't gone very far into the open grassy area away from the balloon when several loud screams rent the air. That was followed by several children crying.

The next thing Polly heard was the roar of a park ranger calling, "Kill that dawg."

Polly didn't hesitate; she headed in the direction of the commotion. Flynn's fists clenched and unclenched as he followed, a frown covering his face.

Soon a huge shaggy dog burst into view, his ears laid back and his legs stretched to their utmost to gain as much speed as possible. His mouth was slobbering and a mangy tail was tucked between his legs.

Polly put out both hands. "Here, doggie," she called in her sweet child's voice. The dog's ears pricked up and he swerved in her direction. As he did so, Flynn stepped in front of Polly, his fists at the ready.

Polly was not to be thwarted and at the last second she merely sidestepped in what Flynn described afterward to the interested servants as the nicest piece of footwork he'd seen in a while. She dropped to her knees and called again as the animal approached.

She thrust both hands about his neck and murmured a little chant about dogs in his ear. The animal's sides were heaving with the effort he'd made to reach her side and he cuddled close, sensing a safe haven in her arms.

Flynn relaxed visibly as he saw the change in the mongrel's demeanor. He knew about mongrels; it was the high-bred dogs the quality owned that he didn't know about, and he would have no trouble with this dog.

Then two park rangers came into view, one brandishing a

cudgel. When they saw Polly with her arms around the dog, they stopped aghast.

"Miss, let that dawg go. 'E's a dangerous animal. 'E's just attacked some little ones." The ranger raised the club as if to strike the dog and the animal growled.

Polly's arms tightened about the dog and she turned pleadingly to Flynn while she murmured soothing words to the dog.

Flynn snatched the club from the man's hand and admonished the man. "We'll 'ave none o' that. 'E doesn't look very nasty to me."

Polly stared into the ranger's face. "I'd like to see the child this dog hurt. It's my opinion that the nursemaid merely got frightened when she saw him trotting toward her charge." She quickly found a name she could use for the dog. "You just wanted to play, didn't you?" She pulled the dog's ears and he assumed the expression of an innocent, long-suffering canine.

The ranger stood his ground. He knew his rights. " 'E's nothing but a mongrel running loose and I'll have to put him down." He tried to explain earnestly to the little face that was appealing to him.

Polly came of strong stock and her mouth firmed with determination. "You can't put him down, as he belongs to me. He just got loose from his leash. I'll take him home and you won't be bothered again." With that she took off the sash around her dress and tied one end around the dog's neck and held the other.

The rangers looked askance at one another, not quite certain what course they ought to pursue, but Flynn took charge. He pulled a couple of gold pieces from his pocket and thrust one into each ranger's hand.

Eyeing the largess with appreciation, both men pocketed the coins and departed.

"Flynn, you're wonderful. How did you happen to have money like that on you?"

Flynn shifted his feet uneasily. "I was given a little sum to carry about with me in case of need." He didn't add that it was Lord Brookfield who gave it to him.

Polly pulled gently on her improvised leash and the dog moved obediently with her, trotting alongside, his head high, as if he were the best-bred animal in the park.

Even Flynn had to smile at the animal's antics. "Miss Polly, what if your sister won't let you keep him?"

Polly looked at him incredulously. "Why how could you think my sister was such a spoilsport? She knows I love pets and here in London I have none. Now I've gotten a splendid one. I'm calling him Lannie. He's the best I've ever owned."

The smile that radiated on her face was so joyful that Flynn gave up the argument.

When Simms opened the door, he stood back in disapproval. "Miss Polly, what's this?"

"Never mind, Simms, it's just my new pet. Where's Sharisse?"

Flynn and Simms exchanged glances, Flynn shrugging his huge shoulders.

"In the small salon," Simms answered in a reluctant tone.

Polly turned and marched down the hall with her new pet. As she entered, she commanded the huge dog to sit and was agreeably surprised when he obeyed, his head nearly as high as she was, his long tongue hanging out in a droll fashion.

Sharisse's eyes grew quite round. "Where did you get that dog, Polly?" Her tone was sharper than she intended and she saw the animal cringe at the sound.

Polly petted him firmly. "The poor thing got into trouble at Green Park and the ranger wanted to do away with him."

Sharisse looked beyond Polly to Flynn, who stood in the doorway.

" 'E's just a mongrel, miss, but 'e seems to have taken a fancy to Miss Polly."

Sharisse stood up and walked around the animal. She noted the large brown eyes and the adoring way he looked at Polly. He was certainly an unkempt mess, but perhaps with a bath and a good trim he might be made to look respectable. However, nothing would change the fact that he was a mongrel. He looked to be part mastiff and part pony. That brought a smile, and seeing it, Polly knew she had cleared the worst hurdle.

"Oh, Sharisse, I knew you'd understand. I'll take him out to the stables and see that he gets a bath."

"Polly, we still have a problem. He's rather large to keep in a London town house and we don't know anything about his house manners."

"If he isn't trained, I'll soon see that he is." Polly's chin showed her determination quite distinctly.

Sharisse sighed, recognizing the signs. "If we can't manage, we'll have to find someone who has a country home not too far away who'll take him and you can visit him there."

Polly frowned. "Come on, Lannie. You're going to have a bath and a trim so you look presentable."

"I'm sorry, miss, but I didn't know what ta do." Flynn's large hands twisted.

"I understand, Flynn, and I don't blame you." She gave him a bit of a smile and picked up the *Gazette* again.

Flynn made for the servants' hall to tell them of the new addition to the household.

Sharisse thought about Polly and the absurd dog and laughed to herself. Mayhap this would keep Polly out of mischief. Surely the dog would be a handful to train.

CHAPTER THIRTEEN

Sharisse was speaking to her housekeeper when Bassett, one of the senior footmen, interrupted. "Miss Sharisse, you have callers, a Sir Vincent James and Lieutenant Michael Sutton. Are you available to receive the visitors?"

Sharisse frowned, trying to place them, but couldn't recollect either one. Her curiosity got the better of her and she instructed the young man, "Please show them to the small salon. Then ask Miss Roberts to join me there directly. Ask Simms to bring in some suitable refreshments in a few minutes."

The young man bowed and withdrew.

Sharisse patted her hair, pinched her already rosy cheeks, and smoothed her lavender afternoon gown. A small bunch of purple pansies adorned each shoulder of the confection and ribbons cascaded down the front and back. She finished her directions to the housekeeper and then made her way leisurely to the salon.

Sir Vincent James looked the room over critically and then turned to his companion. "Everything is of the finest."

Lieutenant Sutton agreed. "I've always wanted to meet an heiress before she got on the town."

"We're stealing a march on the others. Perhaps we can do ourselves some good." His stance bespoke his military background, even if his manner was devious.

"I'm not certain that we're doing the right thing. After all, shouldn't we have someone sponsor us?" Young Sutton seemed uneasy about the business.

Sir Vincent opened his snuffbox and took a pinch, inhaling deeply. "My dear boy, my need of marrying an heiress is much greater than yours and I'm counting on you to help smooth this meeting. When the time comes, I'll grease your wheels accordingly."

Polly was in the next salon, and since the connecting doors weren't tightly closed she could hear the entire conversation. As she heard this her eyes flashed and she whispered to Lannie, "Fortune hunters! Dear Heaven, they're after the money I told Lady Jersey that Sharisse has. What are we going to do to get rid of these two?" She scowled while she set her mind to work and returned to listening to the rest of the conversation.

The man continued. "After all, she's just a little country nobody that happens to have a deal of money and I can use it." Sir Vincent replaced the enameled box in his pocket. "You do know friends of hers, but if we wait for them to get around to introducing us, it might be too late. Someone else might gobble her up," Sir Vincent complained mildly.

"I can well understand your position, but do you think you would want to be shackled to a country bumpkin?" The young man's face showed his uncertainty.

Polly put her eye to the crack in the door to be sure that she could recognize these two when she saw them again, but when she saw Miss Roberts enter the room, she knew that the confidences were at an end and she took herself and Lannie off to the schoolroom.

Both men introduced themselves with a polished air and inquired if Miss Satterleigh were receiving visitors.

Miss Roberts sniffed loudly and replied gravely, "I believe that she is."

Almost on the words, Sharisse swept into the room and made a silent survey of her visitors. Her first response to the older man was one of repugnance, while she felt the younger man had a frank manner that was appealing. "I am Miss Satterleigh. You wished to see me?"

Miss Roberts rocked quietly by the fireplace and watched the proceedings out of partly closed eyes.

After they had introduced themselves, Lieutenant Sutton added, "We're friends of Lord Winchley, and he told us of

Sidney's injury." He paused as if trying to think of what next to say. "We came to express our concern and see if we could help in any way."

Sharisse's eyes began to dance. She knew an excuse when she heard one and this young man seemed to have a deal in common with her little sister. One could always tell when she wanted something. "Thank you for your concern. However, at present we're doing quite well."

Sir Vincent cut in. "We would also like to ask if you are planning to attend Almack's on Friday. I'd like to solicit your hand for the opening dance."

His voice was smooth and his manner ingratiating, but Sharisse discerned more than he would have liked her to. She motioned them to a chair and took one opposite them, while her brain composed excuses. "May I make you known to Miss Roberts, my companion and friend?"

The lady in question merely raised her head and stated firmly, "We've met."

Sharisse was still deciding how best to decline the man's invitation, when Simms trod majestically into the room.

"Lord Brookfield," he announced in stentorian accents.

Inspired, Sharisse said, "You are just in time. Sir Vincent has solicited my hand for the opening dance at Almack's but I was about to tell him that I've already promised it to you."

One of Andrew's eyebrows rose a fraction of an inch and an unholy gleam flashed in his eyes. "Yes, of course, you've been promised to me for some time."

Sharisse had all she could do to keep from gasping and looked quickly at the other two gentlemen to see if they had gleaned what she had from Andrew's remark.

Sir Vincent managed to look disappointed but rallied quickly. "I shall count on a quadrille with you then." He rose to take his leave. "By the way, I was charged to give you a message that Lady Winchley will be calling at her first opportunity."

Lieutenant Sutton managed a shy smile as he stood. "I will look forward to the pleasure of dancing with you also."

As they left, Andrew made his way to Miss Roberts, engaging her in small talk.

"You don't need to spend your time talking to me, young man. I can see that you've more important things on your mind. I'll take myself off and then you two young people can speak plainly." With that she rose and winked at Sharisse before leaving.

Andrew took the offensive. "I'll have you know that that connection won't do. Sir Vincent is a gazetted fortune hunter and I'm at a loss to understand why he has decided to honor you with his presence. As for young Sutton, he's in need of marrying for money, but at least he is a gentleman."

"You mean that Sir Vincent is not? Oh dear, and I found him quite agreeable." She tilted her head provocatively to one side. "I do have to admit it was nice of you to agree to dance with me, for I would have thought you were the last man to attend such a tame gathering as Almack's."

He advanced toward her with a gait that had a decidedly dangerous look to it. "You are so right, my vixen. I never went to Almack's even in my salad days and now I've let you push me into it." He pulled her firmly into his arms. "I think that it's time we came to an understanding, my sweet. I don't like the kind of men you are gathering around you, and the sooner everyone knows I mean you to be mine the better."

She stared into his eyes, trying to determine the exact meaning of his words. Finally she spoke. "You must know I have need to marry someone who is wealthy enough to support Polly and me." Her voice trailed off.

A roguish grin spread across Andrew's face. "And if you found I were as rich as Golden Ball, you'd have me?"

"Golden Ball? I don't believe I ever heard the name." Her face showed her confusion.

"He's probably the wealthiest man in England and he certainly knows it. I don't think he'd appeal to you."

"Now please be serious. If you'll behave yourself and keep your hands off me we might be able to remain friends."

"Never. We're destined to be more than friends."

"Is that so?" she queried jauntily. She was certainly beginning to hope that there was going to be more than just friendship, but he was in need of a severe set-down if he thought she would tamely let him have his way in everything.

Polly pranced into the room with her new pet at her heels. "Oh, I'm sorry. I didn't know you had company. I'd better take Lannie out of here. He doesn't like strangers, especially men."

Andrew gave the huge dog a thorough inspection. "What have you here, Polly? A young pony?" He bent down and snapped his fingers at the dog.

The animal only hesitated for a moment then slowly moved to Andrew's side. When Andrew's strong fingers scratched behind his ears, the mongrel assumed a comical expression of pleasure, making soft sounds in his throat.

Polly looked on in amazement. "I can't understand. When the stableboys tried to wash him he snarled so badly he scared them off and when our head groom tried to put him in the trough he bit him."

"Oh, Polly! We'll be losing all our help." Sharisse's voice held a note of concern.

"Oh no, because it wasn't so bad and I made it right with them besides finishing the job myself." Polly beamed at her resourcefulness.

Sharisse looked at her little sister suspiciously. "And just how did you make it right?"

"I remembered what Flynn did to stop the rangers from trying to kill Lannie. I found a little silver I had put by and gave it to them."

Andrew had to turn away so Sharisse wouldn't see his smile, but his shoulders shook with his mirth and Sharisse noted it with a deal of asperity.

"If Flynn has been teaching you to bribe people, I can see that I'll have to speak with him."

"Please, Sharisse, Flynn and I are friends. I wouldn't want him to know I'd told tales on him." She called Lannie to her and turned to leave. "I'm glad Lannie likes you, Andrew. It makes me like you a little better." With these dampening words she exited, leaving the two remaining occupants convulsed in mirth.

When Andrew could speak again he said engagingly, "I came to take you riding, darling. I know I'm half a day early, but I had the distinct impression that you might like a few minutes out in the fresh air."

"If you'll wait until I can change I'll be happy to accompany you." Sharisse was still smiling and enjoying the comradery of sharing a joke.

"I'll give you ten minutes. There's no need for primping. I like you just as you are." His tone was quite serious but his eyes twinkled their glee.

"Let me take leave to tell you, my lord, that your manners are slipping." Her chin lifted a fraction and she danced from the room as she spoke.

"Just as well you're retreating, for I'll not take that from you, my darling."

His words had a deal of menace in them, but Sharisse merely laughed and ran lightly up the stairs.

Andrew stretched his length in a chair and noted the time with a sly grin. When the ten minutes were almost up he began to pace the floor.

As Sharisse entered the room Andrew had his watch out. He flipped it shut and murmured, "Right on time. I like a woman who is punctual. We're going to deal quite well together."

"You are taking me for granted, Andrew, and I will not have it." She stamped her foot.

"You're fair and far out, my love. I'm having to work harder than I've ever done before to get what I want." His tone was mildly scolding.

Sharisse gazed steadily at him. "Everyone and everything seems to jump to do your bidding, and I'm about to tell you that I won't be part of the retinue."

"I wouldn't expect you to. You're unique and I value you for your intelligence, your quick wit, and your figure. In short, I admire you. You would stand out in a crowd." He watched to see how she reacted to his bold compliments.

"Thank you," she returned stiffly, not quite liking the direction the conversation had taken. She preceded him down the steps and feigned attention to the groom who was holding the horses.

Andrew helped her to mount her mare and they trotted down the cobbled street. When they came to the Hyde Park with its long paths and lovely greenery, they let the horses stretch their legs into a sedate canter.

"I wish that I could have a short gallop. Being held down to a slow canter is not at all my idea of riding."

"It's a good thing you have me along to curtail your desires. You would shock the *ton* with your wild riding."

Sharisse merely nodded, thinking to herself that his presence certainly didn't curb any desires that she had, but she couldn't speak on that subject. It wasn't a proper thing for single females to know about. Of a sudden she found herself with thoughts she'd never entertained before and worrying over a man she hardly knew. It gave her serious pause for thought.

Conversation became light and they enjoyed the ride. Andrew doffed his high-crowned beaver hat each time they met a group of ladies in passing, while Sharisse waved.

Several strolling matrons stopped and watched as Sharisse and Andrew trotted by. It gave Sharisse an uneasy feeling. What was so remarkable?

As they returned to Grosvenor Square, they dismounted and allowed the stableboys to take the horses and walk them up and down the street. Sharisse noted Bassett ushering two ladies out of Satterleigh House. She recognized them at once.

"Belinda and Priscilla—how glad I am to see you. To think I almost missed your call. Please come back in and visit with me."

Andrew raised her hand to his lips and bid her a quick farewell. "I'll see you in the morning."

"I enjoyed the ride." She smiled beguilingly at him before turning to her friends.

The ladies were dressed in the very latest of fashion and

descended the steps to greet her. Sharisse introduced her guests to Andrew and he responded suitably, charming each lady in turn. Then he took his leave, giving them a neat bow.

Belinda gave a curious glance over her shoulder to get a better look at his virile form as he mounted his horse.

"Come, we have lots of time to make up," Sharisse urged and, slipping an arm through her friend's, she drew her into the house. They were comfortably seated in the blue salon when Bassett brought in the tea service with an assortment of biscuits and tiny cucumber sandwiches. Sharisse noted that the young man's service was correct and smooth. It pleased her that Simms had found some capable help to relieve him of the onerous duties.

Priscilla, who looked almost like a Dresden doll, was effervescent. "Pray tell me, how did you happen to meet the famous nabob?"

Belinda gave her stepdaughter a look of reproof but showed her curiosity as well.

Sharisse was startled by Priscilla's question. "What do you mean, nabob? Isn't that the term for someone who has made a fortune in India?"

Priscilla nodded eagerly. "Yes. I heard it on very good authority. You did too, didn't you, Mama?"

Thus appealed to, Belinda reluctantly nodded, watching Sharisse closely as she did so. "He is said to be the catch of the season and all the hostesses are vying with each other to get him to come to their balls and parties."

Sharisse schooled her expression to one of polite interest. "He's a neighbor of ours. I met him when he brought some of Sidney's things home that were left behind in the hurry to ship him out to a first-class hospital."

Belinda's eyes were bright. "It seems he means to keep up the acquaintance."

"Just being friendly. I really know nothing about him except that he's been very helpful."

Priscilla broke in, happy to enlighten her. "I can tell you all about him. I met an old friend of mine in Bond Street when we were shopping and she told me his background."

"Now, Priscilla, we don't gossip." Belinda spoke firmly. "Lord Brookfield is probably an exemplary man."

Priscilla's eyes danced with mischief. "He's had a past that was very exciting and romantic. There was even some doubt about society accepting him again, but with his birth and fortune, he's welcome everywhere."

Belinda raised her hand to quiet the girl.

Sharisse would have liked to hear more, despite the fact that it was gossip, but she didn't want to appear to have more than a passing interest in the man, at least not yet.

Belinda took the conversation in hand. "Will we be seeing you at Almack's? I would be happy to pick you up and act as chaperone for both you and Priscilla."

"How nice it is to have friends. Thank you for the kind offer, and another time I'll probably accept, but on this occasion, Lord Brookfield has offered to escort me and Miss Roberts."

Belinda's eyebrows rose and her eyes grew quite speculative. "However did you manage that? They say he said that Almack's is too flat for him."

"Well, I don't think he was exactly planning to go but circumstances seemed to push him into it." Sharisse grinned as she remembered the scene.

Belinda gave her a sharp look. "I know you, my friend, and I can distinctly detect an odor of fish."

"Mama!" Priscilla was delightfully shocked at her stepmother's expression, but she had to agree that there was something fishy about Sharisse's explanation.

"I have a strong feeling that this season is going to be more lively than I'd thought. I can see I'm going to have my hands full. With Priscilla's presentation and debut and your, shall we say, adventures, I'm certain that I'll have plenty to keep me entertained."

Sharisse gave her friend an innocent grin. "I hope you are not disappointed, Belinda. I am not expecting adventure and romance."

"No," responded her friend gaily, "but it seems to have come looking for you."

Sharisse walked them to the door and kissed each one as they prepared to leave.

Belinda hugged her tightly and whispered, "Remember if you get into a bind, you can count on me."

Sharisse nodded; a lump forming in her throat made it impossible to answer. She waved as the carriage pulled away.

It was a thoughtful Sharisse who climbed the stairs to change for dinner. If Andrew was indeed rich and all the matchmaking mamas were after him, didn't that preclude his being married? She was certain that it did. She sat down at her dresser and dashed off a note to Critchfield. She wanted some answers immediately.

CHAPTER FOURTEEN

Polly scampered down the stairs, Lannie at her heels. The dog had become her shadow over the several days of his residence. "Lannie, sit." A huge grin split her face as the dog responded to her command. "Good dog," she crooned, "you're learning to be such a fine gentleman."

When she heard the front bell, Polly took Lannie to her favorite hiding spot under the stairs so that she could peek and find out who the visitor was without being seen. It had become a game to take note of all Sharisse's callers and decide if the gentlemen were gentlemen or another batch of fortune hunters. Polly had determined to rout the lot.

Simms opened the door and, having no orders to the contrary, admitted Sir Vincent. Polly wrinkled her nose in distaste, but resolutely waited until she saw where Simms put the visitor to wait.

Polly raised Lannie's long nose and pointed a finger warningly at the dog. "Lannie, I'm counting on you to help rid us of this pest. Come along. We've got work to do." Her eyes sparkled their mischief and her step was quite springy.

She marched defiantly into the small salon and told Lannie, "Get him!" and pointed to the figure by the window.

The dog obediently trotted over to where Sir Vincent had been standing, but the man jumped behind a chair for protection.

"Call that brute off," Sir Vincent roared.

When the man raised his voice to Polly the dog began to growl menacingly, baring his teeth.

Polly grinned angelically. "He doesn't seem to want your

company and I don't believe that I find your presence necessary." To the dog she said, "Good dog. Guard!"

"Why, you little devil, I'll get you for this." Fury mottled his complexion and veins stood out in his neck.

Polly advanced to take Lannie's collar. "Better leave while you can," she advised coolly. "I don't know how long I can control him."

Sir Vincent's gaze shifted from the growling dog to the open door, but no relief seemed to be in sight. He pointed a finger at Polly. "Don't think that you'll get away with this." The menace in his voice was distinct.

Lannie's ears lay back and he barked, straining at Polly's grasp. "My hand's slipping." Polly's face mirrored her delight.

Sir Vincent didn't hesitate any longer. As the dog seemed to erupt from Polly's hand, he made a dash for the door and flung it shut behind him, heaving a heartfelt sigh of relief as he did so. With a quick scan of the hall and the stairs, he determined that Sharisse's entrance wasn't imminent and discretion won the better part of valor.

Sharisse descended into the front hall a few moments later and found Polly standing there grinning. "Your visitor just left," announced Polly baldly.

"That's odd. Was something the matter?"

"Not anymore," Polly murmured quietly. Then she looked up consideringly and smiled brightly. "I don't believe that the man likes children. I don't think he'll come back."

Sharisse searched her sister's face. "Polly, did you do something to upset him?"

"I didn't, but he seemed to take exception to Lannie." She patted the dog's large head and smiled at her pet.

Lannie's tongue lolled, his tail wagged, and his posture was that of a pattern card of virtue.

Sharisse studied the animal for a few seconds and shook her head in bewilderment. "That dog wouldn't attack anyone. He doesn't have a mean bone in his body. I daresay that he wouldn't even growl at a kitten."

"How about a mouse?" Polly inquired with an inquisitive grin.

"You're making Sir Vincent sound a very poor spirit," she complained jestingly.

"No, I don't think he has any," Polly said solemnly.

Then both girls burst out in strong laughter. Sharisse shook her head in mirth while Polly doubled over.

When they had calmed a bit, Sharisse tried another tack to the conversation. "I'm going to Almack's tomorrow evening, and of course Robbie will accompany me. You'll have all the servants to keep you company, so I'm sure you can manage. Do you mind?" Her voice showed a small trace of anxiety, as this was her first evening excursion and would leave Polly without her company.

"You needn't worry. I have Lannie and if there's any trouble he'll take care of me." She pulled the dog's ears fondly and he rubbed against her, his weight almost tipping her over.

"Fine lot of good he'd be! I've never seen so gentle a dog." Sharisse sniffed deprecatingly.

"But you didn't see him in the park when the ranger was about to attack him or when the groom tried to put him in the horse trough to wash him. He has an impressive set of teeth."

Sharisse gave her coif a last pat and adjusted one sleeve of the emerald green evening gown with lace gauze overdrape. She decided to forgo wearing a necklace, thinking the lace inset about the neck was sufficiently elaborate and displayed her creamy skin to advantage.

A knock on her door informed her that Lord Brookfield had arrived and she draped a lace shawl about her shoulders. When she entered the drawing room, she found Andrew speaking to a glowing Miss Roberts. Andrew was complimenting the older woman on her choice of gowns.

Miss Roberts had chosen a dove gray gown in the Empire style with Alençon lace. It suited her exactly, with its subdued color and restrained trim. "I thank you, Lord Brookfield. Sharisse helped me to select the fashion plate to have it made up from." She nodded in Sharisse's direction, at which Andrew turned around.

His eyes softened and a broad smile lit his face as he studied her appearance. "I daresay that I have the pleasure of escorting the two most elegant ladies to arrive at Almack's this evening."

Sharisse approved of Andrew's black coat of Bath superfine and his sparkling white small clothes and elegant knee breeches. The white seemed to draw attention to his swarthy complexion in an interesting way and Sharisse found she admired everything about this man. Her stomach had a knot in it that radiated a deal of heat, and her pulse speeded its rhythm.

Andrew picked something up from one of the small tables in the room and held it out to her. "This is for you."

As she unwrapped it, she found it was a tiny corsage of yellow rosebuds. It would be perfect with her dress and as she picked it up to examine it, she noted the jeweled clasp to pin it on her gown. Reluctantly she handed the flowers back. "I can't take jewelry from you."

He just shook his head and smiled, taking it from her hands and pinning it on her right shoulder. Then he stood back and smiled, quite satisfied with his handiwork.

Sharisse tapped her foot and exclaimed, "Everyone will assume that we have an understanding between us."

"That's a comforting thought," Andrew replied readily, his smile growing broader. "I'd like to be able to think that you understand me exceedingly well when the proper time comes." His eyes danced with merriment and a flame of passion seemed to emanate from them.

Sharisse was at a loss as to how to answer the man. He seemed to be intimating a future, but the last time she had accused him of such, she'd suffered a slight rebuff. She wasn't about to make a cake of herself twice, so she kept her thoughts quiet.

Andrew took her hand. "Come, let's cry truce. I won't tell where your posies came from if you won't." Then he assisted both ladies out to his waiting carriage.

As Sharisse entered the ballroom on Andrew's arm, she noted that the surroundings hadn't changed much since she'd been here last. Again the ladies were a rainbow of colors, each one trying to outdo the others. The gentlemen seemed to have an abundance of jewelry and she contrasted them to Andrew's quiet elegance. His black and white was startling in such a riot of color, and it suited him perfectly.

Lord Brookfield procured a card for her and then found a seat for Miss Roberts in the corner of the room with several of the older matrons and gentleman.

When Sharisse looked at her dance card she found Andrew's name scrawled across the first and last dances.

At her inquiring expression he shrugged his shoulders. "I'd like to scratch my name across the whole program, but it would single you out for too much attention, so I'll have to be content to play the gentleman this evening."

"Oh, you mean you intend at some time in the future not to act like a gentleman?" she inquired saucily as they strolled about the room.

"None of the male species are gentlemen all the time, my sweet, and you'll do well to remember it." His eyes caressed her softly and she gazed questioningly into them.

"I don't believe that I understand your meaning, my lord." Her heart fluttered within her breast and she thought her face might have a telltale flush.

"We'll discuss it at a more propitious time, darling. Do you see any of your friends yet?"

"Yes, Priscilla and Belinda are over by that potted fern. Could we stop and speak with them?" She waved as she caught the ladies' attention.

Soon there was a throng of people about them and Sharisse found herself much sought after. When she looked up to see what Andrew was about, she found that there were several of the most important matrons and their respective daughters vying for his attention.

Sharisse found she was almost jealous of the fawning attention that he was receiving. She sighed philosophically. At least whatever peccadillos he'd committed as a young man were evidently being swept under the carpet and forgotten. His birth and breeding were impeccable, but others had been shunned in spite of those qualities. It was usually money, a great deal of money, that was responsible for such a welcome and it gave Sharisse pause for thought.

The musicians finished tuning up and the master of ceremonies welcomed the assemblage and announced the first dance. Andrew led her out into the first set. She performed her part of the figures with an easy grace and noted that Andrew managed quite creditably. As the movement of the dance took her from his side, Sir Vincent moved forward and bowed charmingly.

"Save me the first waltz," he whispered suavely before he danced on past.

Sharisse smiled benevolently. He wouldn't get the chance. When she was here previously, she had been such a mouse that she had never received official approval from the patronesses for the waltz. Until she did so, it would be social suicide to attempt the dance, and her smile broadened as she thought of foiling the man again.

Andrew caught her hand as the steps brought them together again and noted her expression. "What mischief are you contemplating, my darling? It is written all over your charming face."

"Nothing to do with you, my lord," she replied pertly.

His eyes narrowed thoughtfully. "Don't try my patience too far, my love. I'm not noted for it."

She laughed delightedly, causing her next partner to raise his brows in surprise. It was quite unusual for young ladies to laugh so joyously at Almack's.

Sharisse sought out Priscilla and asked, "Are you finding something to keep yourself amused?"

Priscilla smiled and commented, "I see that you are quite sought after this evening, as is Lord Brookfield. Even Lady Ambersly is making a push to introduce her daughter."

"Then it is true that he has a great deal of money?" Sharisse asked quietly. She studied her friend's face, a slight frown marring her countenance.

"Why, yes. We told you that some time ago. Didn't you believe Belinda?"

"I thought it might be just gossip that had ballooned into far more than the original story." She bit her lip in consternation. She did not wish anyone to think she was setting her cap at a fortune.

"Don't worry, Sharisse. Things have a way of working out for the best. Lord Brookfield seems a sensible man to me." Priscilla spoke in a comforting tone and she chafed her friend's hand.

"How do I know if he's serious or just amusing himself? The thought whirls about my head hour after hour," she whispered, her face stretched into the social smile required at these affairs.

Priscilla looked knowingly at Sharisse and nodded her head as if to confirm a suspicion. "Try setting up a flirtation with another gentleman and see how he reacts. I have never seen one yet that won't react in some way to another encroaching upon his territory."

Sharisse nodded and her smile grew appreciably. When her next partner came to claim her, she was the soul of vivacity and laughter. She searched the room for a likely recipient of her flirtation and her eyes stopped upon Sir Vincent. Sharisse had no compunction about using the man, for his whole personality was a façade. She'd always been able to separate the honest admirers from the coxcombs and sharps. It was only Andrew who seemed to mystify her. She had tried to decipher that puzzle, but hadn't been able to make much headway.

Several dances and partners flew by as Sharisse allowed herself to enjoy the movements and conversations. As the musicians struck up the first waltz, she tensed a bit, knowing that she was going to have to fend off Sir Vincent.

"May I have this dance, Miss Satterleigh?" Sir Vincent inquired politely.

"I don't believe that I care to waltz, thank you." Sharisse

eyed the man with distaste but tried to overcome her hesitancy.

"Is it possible that one of the patronesses hasn't given you her sanction yet?" His tone was incredulous.

"I wasn't much interested in dancing when I last came, Sir Vincent," she replied in an apologetic manner.

"I shall remedy the situation immediately." He threw his shoulders back in a gesture of self-importance and then took her arm with a deal of ceremony. He walked her to where the patronesses were seated and asked quite formally, "Lady Lieven, may I present Miss Satterleigh?" He bowed with respect and seemed to all who witnessed the event, a prince by manner.

Sharisse noted several admiring looks from young ladies but couldn't bring herself to be suitably impressed.

Countess Lieven was seated next to Mrs. Burrell and both ladies smiled warmly at the man. "Dear Sir Vincent, I have already made Sharisse's acquaintance. I'm happy to see you have too."

"Then may I ask for your approval of Miss Satterleigh to dance the waltz?" He gave his most winning smile and waited patiently.

The countess turned to her friend and asked, "Shall we allow Miss Satterleigh to waltz?"

Mrs. Burrell pursed her lips for a moment while she studied Sharisse's attire and then nodded her assent.

The countess stood up for a moment and uttered the magic words. "Miss Satterleigh, may I present Sir Vincent as an eligible partner for this dance?"

Sharisse adroitly thanked the patroness and then let Sir Vincent lead her onto the floor. She wondered what Andrew would be thinking, as he hadn't solicited her hand for a waltz.

Sir Vincent led her about the room with the grace of a member of the Russian ballet. Many sighs followed the couple as they twirled gracefully around the ballroom floor and Sharisse found her first experience with the waltz, other than in the ballroom at Satterleigh House with a music instructor helping her with the steps, exhilarating and enjoyable.

When the dance concluded her partner took her hand. "May I ask for your company for a ride in the park tomorrow?"

Sharisse was about to plead another engagement when her eyes caught Andrew's and he frowned fiercely at her.

Sir Vincent cut in smoothly. "You owe me something for failing to wear my flowers. May I ask who is the lucky man?"

Sharisse stared appraisingly at Andrew's scowling countenance from across the room and decided that indeed it would do him a deal of good to think he had some competition. "A dear friend gave them to me."

"You aren't going to give me his name, then?" It was apparent to those who knew him he was irritated, but Sharisse didn't discern it, for she couldn't interpret that muscle twitch in his cheek.

"No, I don't believe that I am." She grinned merrily. "Let me assure you that yours isn't the only posy to grace my table this evening, but I shall enjoy looking at it. Thank you for sending such lovely flowers. Would nine be a suitable hour for our ride?"

He nodded happily and kissed her hand lightly. That seemed to mollify the man and at her request he escorted her to a chair.

Sharisse was piqued when Andrew didn't rush to utter his disapproval and so she threw herself willy-nilly into the gaiety of the evening. Andrew had his hands full fending off the advances of encroaching mamas and leading overly shy daughters onto the floor.

When Sir Vincent came to claim her hand for a second waltz, Sharisse caught a glimpse of irritation on Andrew's face before he schooled it into polite disdain. As she walked onto the floor, she smiled far more warmly than she would have normally. Sir Vincent seemed to be quite satisfied with her as his partner and was at pains to entertain her with the latest *on dits*.

Sharisse laughed in the appropriate places and forced herself to appear to be having a delightful conversation. When Andrew danced by with one of the season's prettiest debutantes, Sharisse herself knew a moment of intense jealousy. The girl gazed up adoringly at Lord Brookfield and hung upon his every word.

A rush of blood made Sharisse's chest burn and she had difficulty controlling her breathing but, with Sir Vincent eyeing her warily, offered tightly, "It's a bit warm in here, don't you think?"

"Ah, my dear, I believe that it's just the vivacity of the dance. You'll get used to it. Mark my words." He nodded consolingly.

Sharisse almost burst out laughing, the tension completely relieved. Sir Vincent thought himself the last word on every subject, and again proved that he was far wide of the mark.

By the time Lord Brookfield came to claim her hand for the last dance, Sharisse was quite ready to call the evening to a close. He grasped her firmly and executed the required movements of the country dance. "How did you come to waltz twice with that macaroni?"

"Wasn't it thoughtful of Sir Vincent to see that I was approved by the patronesses to waltz? And he dances so divinely." She cocked her head to one side and waited for the storm to erupt.

A vein stood out down Andrew's temple and his face darkened. "The man's a gazetted fortune hunter and toadies to all the patronesses to get what he wants. He's not fit to clean your chimney," he growled in a strong whisper.

Sharisse, not content with the anger she'd drawn, added another element to the storm. "Wasn't it kind of him to offer to take me riding tomorrow?" She managed to make her query in an innocent tone and was inordinately pleased with the results.

"You have a few facts to learn in the near future, my darling, and I intend to do the educating." His voice was filled with determination, while his face showed a touch of exasperation.

The pattern of the dance separated them and Sharisse

wasn't obliged to reply for a time but merely smiled benevolently. When the dance concluded and Lord Brookfield escorted her to find Miss Roberts, Sharisse murmured coolly, "I believe that I am quite capable of discerning facts for myself, my lord, and I will not be bullied by you or anyone else."

"That point remains to be seen, my charming vixen. You present me with a challenge that I find I can not resist."

CHAPTER FIFTEEN

Bassett knocked on Sharisse's door to inform her that Sir Vincent had arrived. She put on tan leather riding gloves after making a last assessment in front of the mirror. Her habit was of canary yellow and a tan ostrich plume curled from the side of her hat. Her boots were of soft kid molded to a nicely turned ankle.

Polly had been on the lookout for Sir Vincent, and as he entered she put both hands on her hips and stared fiercely. "Do I have to call Lannie?"

Sir Vincent gazed at the small figure with contempt. "You are talking mighty tall for such a small girl. It might be wise to tread softly. One never knows when one will meet trouble unexpectedly."

"Are you going to leave?" When the man persisted in waiting, she began to call, "Lannie, here boy. Lannie!"

Sir Vincent gave her a malevolent glare and went huffily out the door.

When Sharisse came down to the entry hall she found Polly there playing with the dog, a satisfied expression on her face.

"Where is Sir Vincent? I understood that he had come."

"Yes, he was like the wind. He came and went."

Sharisse went out to see if he were waiting outside. "Why didn't you wait for me inside?"

He licked his lips in an unconscious manner and explained apologetically, "I found a sudden need to enjoy the warmth of the day. The house seemed a bit chilly."

Sharisse settled her skirts gracefully over the sidesaddle and gave her hat a last pat to be certain it was firmly on her head. With a dig of her heel, she led the way toward Hyde Park.

Sir Vincent regaled her with the latest bits of court gossip and attempted to make himself a pleasant companion. His eyes frequently darted at his companion to see how his remarks were being received.

Sharisse smiled benevolently. She had no problem with her conscience in turning the tables on this fellow. He deserved all he got and probably more than she planned upon dishing out. She pulled up her horse quickly when she saw Belinda.

"Hello!" She beckoned her friends to join them.

Sir Vincent watched speculatively.

When Belinda and her stepdaughter had maneuvered their horses to facilitate conversation, Sharisse made the necessary introductions and then asked lightly, "Belinda, will you be at home this afternoon? I have a . . . recipe that I'd like your opinion of."

"Why, yes, we'll be available. Is this perhaps concerning the ingredients we spoke of at Almack's last night?"

Sharisse nodded, her eyes exchanging knowing glances with her friend. Belinda wished them a pleasant ride and she and Priscilla set off down one of the other paths.

Resolutely Sharisse turned her attention to her companion and local events of the day. "Did you happen to note the cartoon in yesterday's *Gazette?* The work was superior to that of the others I've seen. I was quite taken with the comic features of the Regent and the detail of the drawing."

"It's not a fitting subject for comedy. I found the entire subject in poor taste. The Regent should not be a topic of household censure." The man spoke at his most pious.

"I am certain that your thoughts on the subject do you credit, Sir Vincent." Sharisse held her inward grin and looked for more innocuous topics.

As she entered Satterleigh House, pulling off her riding gloves, Lannie waited patiently at the door. "You're a fraud, you know," she told the animal.

Polly appeared and patted the dog almost reverently. "Did you have a nice ride?"

"It was amusing. I met Belinda and Priscilla in the park and have made arrangements to go visit them after nuncheon. Would you like to go along?"

Polly's face brightened and she tilted it to one side pleadingly. "Yes, if you'll let me take Lannie along." She finished her performance with a pout that she used to get her cookies from cook.

"Polly, we can't make a social call with a animal that size." She had a hard time keeping her face devoid of emotion, though the thought of the huge animal in Belinda's parlor was clearly funny.

"Priscilla likes dogs and she'd enjoy meeting Lannie."

"Very well, but if he doesn't mind his manners, he'll remain in the stables while we visit."

Polly's face was wreathed in smiles. "Thank you, Rissy. Now I know we'll have a splendid time."

When the groom brought around the matched pair of chestnuts, Sharisse held out her hand. "I'll take them, Ned." She accompanied her command with a generous smile.

Polly jumped in, Lannie at her heels.

"We are going to be a bit crowded besides having everyone in London seeing us making cakes of ourselves."

"What a bag of moonshine. As if you cared what people think. We're supposed to be ourselves. Isn't that what you've always told me?"

Sharisse didn't have any defense against that remark. Her chickens had come home to roost. With a laugh she guided her pair through the streets, oblivious to the stares they received.

When they pulled up at Winchley House, a servant ran down the stairs to take the horses, giving Lannie an astonished look, but he was far too well trained to offer a comment.

The butler greeted them with a deal of reserve, eyeing the large animal between them. He permitted himself to greet them and usher them into one of the small salons. Priscilla bounced into the room almost immediately, while Belinda followed at a more sedate pace.

"Polly, where did you find such a splendid dog?" Priscilla patted the dog's head adoringly.

"I knew you would want to meet him. He can do several tricks." Polly beamed her pride.

"Let's take him out to the garden." She turned to Sharisse. "Would that be acceptable to you, Sharisse?"

Sharisse nodded her approval, but Belinda was clearly having trouble containing her mirth.

"Belinda, as long as Priscilla and Polly have something to entertain them for a while, would you care for a turn around the park to get a bit of fresh air?"

She cast her friend a speculative glance. "Ah yes, the recipe."

Both girls laughed and went in search of Belinda's bonnet and gloves.

The wind whipped against their faces as their carriage rolled through the park at a spanking pace. "I received a letter from my solicitor this morning, confirming that Lord Brookfield is indeed single and, moreover, that he is one of the richest men in all England."

Belinda raised her hands in a gesture of confusion. "What troubles you, then?"

"I have no wish to be thought to be setting my cap at a fortune."

"Surely that can't weigh much with you. Lord Brookfield is a fine man, from what I've seen of him."

"I have quite another larger set of problems. I haven't told a soul and I am trusting you to keep this piece of information in the strictest confidence—not even telling Priscilla or your husband."

"Sharisse, you wound me. Of all things you know that I stand buff against that sort of thing. Look at the adventures we shared as schoolgirls and neither of us told." Her voice held a note of complaint and hurt.

"It's just that this is so serious. Sidney was killed in a native battle in India some weeks ago. There is no provision in the will for Polly or me, and I can't think that even if Margaret has Sidney's heir they will part with a living for us."

"I take it that you haven't turned the letter over to the solicitor yet?"

"That's right. I thought that if I could keep the facts submerged for a time, I might find a husband who would keep both Polly and me." She sighed wearily.

"But, Sharisse, that's just what you've got in Lord Brookfield."

"You don't understand. There's also the question of Polly. She seems to have taken a strange aversion to every gentleman who comes to the house. She pulled several of her pranks on Lord Brookfield and I believe that she's starting on Sir Vincent. I think that it might be best if I practice a strict economy, tuck money away against my future needs, and when the truth can't be hidden any longer, just retire to the country estate in Gloucester. It is small and no one has been there for years. I doubt that Margaret will be interested in it."

"Sharisse, I can't make up your mind for you, but if you want my opinion, and I assume that's what you've come for, I think you ought to accept his offer when the time comes."

"What if he finds when he hears what I've done that he can't abide me any longer? I would rather die than to be put in such a position."

"It is a problem, but I think that you wrong Lord Brookfield. If you told him of your dilemma, might he not be forgiving?"

"I don't know." They set the horses toward Winchley House and Sharisse contemplated her friend's advice.

When they reached Pall Mall they saw several children playing in the street. They darted in and out in front of vehicles in some sort of game. Sharisse had pulled the horses to a walk, when a milk wagon and driver swerved out of a side street and into the crowd. The off front leg of one of the large draft horses hit one of the smaller children and the child fell to the cobbled stone flagway, blood streaming from his head.

The driver of the wagon shouted imprecations as he swung his heavy wagon around the child and continued on. Those on the sidewalks stopped to look, but no one offered to help.

Sharisse had stopped the phaeton and thrust the reins into

her friend's hands. She disentangled her skirts from the carriage and made her way to the boy. She used a clean kerchief from her reticule to wipe the blood and assess the damage to the child's face. When she had time to look up, she saw several fashionable vehicles pass by and her anger was kindled.

A familiar voice cut her short. "Having a spot of trouble, darling?"

She sat back on her heels and gazed at Andrew with a sigh of heartfelt relief. Without another word he swung down beside her and handed her his reins. "Hold them for me while I put the lad in my curricle."

She watched as he gently raised the boy in his arms and placed him on the cushioned seat.

Sharisse's heart warmed. "Andrew, I want to come with you to find the boy a doctor."

His eyebrows raised as he surveyed her blood-spattered attire. "Are you certain you want to do this?" He then gestured to the approaching carriages.

"I'm not going to let the opinion of a few stop me from doing my duty." She turned back to Belinda. "Do you think that you can drive the carriage back to Winchley House and let me pick it up later?"

Her friend smiled at her and Lord Brookfield. "I'll be happy to assist in any way I can. And, Sharisse, I believe that your recipe is going to taste better than you envision it." She smiled at Andrew and winked outrageously at her friend, then flicked the reins.

The crowd was dissipating now that the excitement was over. Andrew looked up and down the street. "Sir Robert Peel is right! We need a better method for law and order. There's never a constable about when you need one."

The boy moaned as he regained consciousness in Sharisse's arms. "You're going to be fine, young man."

"Please, ma'am, let me go. I didn't do nothing." He was shaking badly and Sharisse assumed it was more from fright than injury.

"I know you didn't, but you need a stitch or two in your head."

The child began to thrash wildly. "I can't. M' ma's not got any of the ready t' pay."

"No one is asking you to. We'll take care of it and then drive you home."

Andrew's expression softened as he stole a glance at Sharisse and the boy. "You have taken the words from my mouth, my darling. How well we shall deal together. You speak the truth without varnishing it. I required that in my woman."

The words hurt her extraordinarily and tears began to sting her eyes. Here was the answer she had been waiting for. With a gesture of inevitability, she dashed the tear from her cheek and began to occupy the boy's attention with stories.

Sir Vincent rapped the knocker sharply on the door at Satterleigh House, a sly smile on his face. "Now we shall see, Miss Polly, who gets the last card."

Bassett opened the door and admitted him. "I'm sorry to say that Miss Satterleigh is not at home."

"Well then, I'd like a word with Miss Polly." His voice held a deal of hauteur and it hit its mark.

"Miss Polly and her dog went with her. Would you care to leave a message?"

"Could you provide me with some writing paper?"

The footman nodded and let the way to one of the rear salons that had a writing table.

"You will find quills and paper in the drawer." As Sir Vincent sat down, he withdrew and allowed the man a few minutes of privacy to compose the letter.

Sir Vincent jumped up, taking a note out of his pocket and put it on the desk. Walking about the room, he peered under and behind the furniture. When he came to the old high-back chair set in the corner, more for looks than for sitting, he smiled with satisfaction. Reaching into his coat pocket, he extracted something shiny and a piece of court plaster and taped the article to the bottom.

When Bassett returned, Sir Vincent was capping the ink and picking up the letter. "Thank you, young man. I appreciate your help. Would you be so kind as to give this to Miss Satterleigh when she returns?" He accompanied the request with a coin.

"Very good, sir."

Sir Vincent left with a triumphant air, his chest thrusting forward and a sly smirk on his face.

Andrew ushered Sharisse into Winchley House.

Belinda eyed her guests critically, assessing the situation. "Sharisse, may I take you upstairs to freshen up? You'll excuse us won't you, Lord Brookfield?" Without waiting for an answer, she whisked Sharisse from the hall and up the curved stairs.

"Sharisse, doesn't his behavior in the circumstances warrant rethinking your decision?" Belinda watched the troubled eyes consolingly.

"He said that the thing he admired best about me is my directness in telling the truth! He would never, never forgive me for deceiving him so."

"Oh," was the only comment Belinda could utter. Sharisse's remark had stunned her.

When the ladies descended to the salon, Andrew was looking out the window with his hands clasped behind his back. Hearing their entrance, he turned, and as he did so Belinda noted how his eyes softened to a distinct tenderness as they rested upon Sharisse. She pursed her lips in thought.

"There now, I'm not so bad, am I?" Sharisse asked.

"Fishing, my darling? There's no need. To me you are Venus, Athena, and Diana all in one."

Sharisse blushed to the roots of her hair, while Belinda hid a beaming smile behind a slight cough.

"Belinda, would you call for my phaeton and the girls?"

Lord Brookfield spoke up. "I have no intention of permitting you to drive. You've had enough in your dish for one day. I'll drive you and Polly home. Lady Winchley, would you see that Sharisse's carriage is returned to her stables?"

"Certainly, I'd be delighted," was the prompt reply. She tugged on the bell pull and issued her orders in a quiet voice. Then she went across the hall to call the girls.

Sharisse was about to utter a denial of the necessity of Andrew's offer, when she remembered Lannie. Laughing with the absurdity of the image that came to mind, she determined that the best way to stuff his loaf was to demur to his wishes.

"Is there some joke I missed, Sharisse?" Andrew queried, raising an eyebrow.

"No, I promise you'll see soon enough."

"Sharisse, I wish that you would walk out to the garden and peek outside. Polly and Priscilla have something to show you." Belinda gestured toward the door.

Sharisse looked from her friend to Andrew and excused herself.

Belinda began, "Lord Brookfield, I hope that you'll forgive my plain speaking, but I believe that you have a decided partiality for Sharisse. Am I correct?"

"I don't see how it concerns you, Lady Winchley." His voice was stiff.

"I am certain that I am right and that your affections are returned. My assessment of the situation is this. Sharisse is afraid that certain circumstances of her past will make her unacceptable."

"Rubbish. She must know that I don't give a fig for her past. I have my own to live down."

"Just as I thought. Be kind to her. She is my dearest friend."

At that moment Sharisse walked in with the girls and Lannie, all joking about the dog's antics.

"And I thought we were crowded taking Tom home," sighed Andrew, and ushered the entourage to his waiting curricle.

"I'd adore a sketch of this. I could use it for blackmail." Belinda grinned widely as she watched the occupants of the carriage shuffle to gain some room.

"I am glad that we don't have far to go," said Andrew. As a stylish carriage swung into view he added, "Our credit is about to be taxed to the utmost." He waved a farewell to Belinda and Priscilla and flicked the reins.

As they wended their way through the traffic, Polly turned to Sharisse. "What's blackmail?"

"It's something that dishonest people do to control others," Andrew offered.

"I don't understand," complained Polly.

"The simplest way to explain it, Polly, is to say that it's knowing information that can hurt someone or having power that can hurt someone and threatening the person to make him do what the blackmailer wants." Sharisse spoke softly and her arms tightened about her sister.

"You mean that Belinda could blackmail you by saying that she'll tell everyone how we look and we wouldn't like it?"

"That's correct, Polly." Andrew winked at the little girl. "If she were blackmailing us, then she would say that if we did whatever it was that she wanted, she wouldn't tell."

"Oh, I see. Well, that's not going to happen to us!" Polly's voice rang with conviction.

"I don't think you'll have to worry about it, either of you, but if anyone threatens you, come to me. I'll settle the matter."

CHAPTER SIXTEEN

They pulled up in front of Satterleigh House just as a very rotund gentleman passed, riding a showy white gelding. Turning to take a second astonished look, he almost lost his seat. "I say . . ."

Sharisse averted her eyes and covered her mouth to hide her amusement, but failed miserably.

"You abominable wretch!" exclaimed Andrew. "That gentleman was the Marquis of Camenfort and he's a high stickler. I wonder how I'm going to explain my lapse?"

"My advice is, don't. Never explain. It's a sign of weakness." She chuckled out loud, her large brown eyes twinkling.

"Clever." He considered the matter for a moment. "A valuable lesson. One that suits my purpose."

As they wandered into the front hall, Bassett came forward. "Sir Vincent called and left you this message."

Polly trotted off with Lannie as Sharisse took the letter. After a quick glance at Andrew, she motioned him to follow her to the green salon. She opened the letter carelessly. There were only two lines inviting her to attend Lady Englethorpe's ball with him.

Andrew, whose eyes had narrowed to slits on hearing the missive was from Sir Vincent, didn't hesitate and pulled the sheet from her fingers, acquainting himself with the message. "Well, he's out there. I have already spoken first and if you didn't make your appearance under my escort my Aunt Englethorpe would rake me over the coals."

"I don't care to be ordered about." Her voice held a haughty note.

"We're not going to play games, my darling. I shall trust you to remember that you are mine."

"You certainly mistake the matter if you think that I'll drop into your lap like some ripe plum."

"Never that," he returned. "More like a tart peach waiting to be sweetened by warmth and care."

"I'll have you know that others find me quite acceptable as I am." Fire danced in her eyes and her fingers drummed on her folded arms.

"I wouldn't want you to change. I never know what to expect next. You are a constant source of amusement." His countenance reflected his growing passion.

Sharisse stepped back. "Thank you for making me sound like some sideshow freak. I should have suspected that I was a novelty to you."

"Is that a subtle way to ask what you are to me?" He scanned her suddenly serious face, his countenance warming as he drew her into his arms. "You are the center of my universe, my guiding star. I chart my course by your radiating beauty."

Sharisse had received her share of compliments during her previous season, but nothing had prepared her for this and she listened raptly, her breathing growing shallow and rapid, her pulse beginning to race. Her eyes seemed to focus on the descending lips that captured hers and she sighed.

Andrew tantalizingly tasted the depths of her mouth and cradled her against his hard length. His large hands sought out the soft curves of her hip and waist, wreaking havoc with her senses.

Sharisse melted under the onslaught and her knees gave way. She held on to him as if the world were falling away at her feet and he was the only secure haven. A soft meow issued from her throat as he deepened the kiss, ravaging the dark recesses, claiming her for his own. That was the right word, she thought frantically, she felt completely claimed. She must get away from him before she destroyed what creditability she had left. She began to struggle and Andrew set her from him slowly, relishing the disarray and confused yearning he saw stamped upon her.

"Andrew, let me go. You mustn't do this to me. I'm not that kind of woman." She was gasping for air and she sounded unsure.

"My darling, I have a secret to tell you," he whispered teasingly. "Every woman is that kind with the right man. For you that is me, only me." He spoke with a possessiveness that bespoke the depth of his feelings.

"It is not meant to be, Andrew."

The words were a plea for understanding, but he saw them as another barrier to cross, especially in the light of Belinda's remarks. "Don't you think that you could accept an offer from a man with a background like mine?"

"It's not that at all! It's just that . . ." Her voice grew agitated and tears trickled down her cheeks. She shook her head as if to clear it and then took a deep breath. "I can't talk about it. You'll just have to accept the fact that it is not to be."

"You can't mean that after allowing me to make love to you in this fashion, darling," he complained teasingly. "You have compromised me and I shall demand something be done about it."

Suddenly she began to laugh. The man was absurd with his hurt looks and outrageous remarks. It was one of the things she liked best about him. He could defuse almost any tense situation. "I must go, Andrew." Her eyes held his and for a time neither spoke, their gazes sending messages to and fro.

"We'll speak of this again another time, darling. Right now I don't think I'm up to arguing. I'll be here to pick you up at seven tomorrow to go to dinner at my aunt's before her ball."

Sir Vincent rapped the knocker loudly, trying to arrange his predatory face in a semblance of politeness. He asked for Miss Satterleigh.

Simms answered the call and announced loftily, "If you'd care to wait in the small salon, I'll inquire." He led the man down the hall.

Polly, Lannie, and Flynn trooped through the back hall and met him almost at the entrance to the salon. Simms, after seeing that Polly wanted a word with the man, went in search of Sharisse.

Sir Vincent's face was white but he redoubled his determination. "I have something I'd like to speak to you about, Miss Polly. Tell this bruiser to hold that animal while we talk for a few minutes."

Flynn frowned but couldn't fault the plan, as he'd no intention of removing from sight. He nodded and took the dog to the front door.

"I want you to speak with your sister on my behalf and tell her that I would make a good husband and that you like me," he commanded in a hushed tone.

"And why should I do that? I *don't* like you and neither does Lannie."

"Because if you don't call off your dog and make me welcome, I'll see that she's accused of stealing a very expensive ring of mine. She'll have to go to the Old Bailey and stand trial. The best she can get is to be transported, although they usually hang for an offense as serious as this."

Polly listened intently, her eyes narrowing thoughtfully. When he finished, she exclaimed softly, "That's blackmail!"

At the sound of Polly's voice, Lannie started to growl. Flynn held a restraining hand on the dog's collar, but he called, "You 'ave need o' me, Miss Polly?"

"No. I was just surprised." She turned her attention to a grim Sir Vincent.

"You can never prove that. Everybody knows my sister."

"Ah, but I can prove it. I've hidden my ring in your house in a place you'll never find. When I bring the constables in I'll be able to point out the right direction if they don't come up with it on their own."

"How long do I have to think this over?" She scowled fiercely.

"Tomorrow is Lady Englethorpe's ball and all the world will

be there. You take her aside between now and then and convince her to accept my offer of marriage."

"What happens if I can't convince her?"

"Then she will have to take the consequences, so you'd better be very, very persuasive, Polly." His feral eyes gleamed as he made the threat.

Polly ran to join Flynn and Lannie. "Let's go for a walk," she almost cried. She gave Sir Vincent one last look of contempt and flung herself out the door.

Sir Vincent sauntered into the small salon like a man who had just been told he'd gained a fortune.

Sharisse reluctantly entered the room. "What may I do for you this morning, Sir Vincent? I'm quite busy today."

"I'm sorry to trouble you, and I won't keep you long. "I came for an answer to my invitation to Lady Englethorpe's ball."

Sharisse assessed the bland face with detached interest. The man should have been an actor. He was quite good at masking his true emotions. "Thank you kindly, but I have already accepted another invitation. I will probably see you there."

He looked suitably crestfallen. "Then I shall have to make do with dancing with you several times. I hope that you'll honor me with a couple of waltzes again. You dance it so delightfully."

"It was generous of you to see that I was approved by the patronesses and I see no reason that I can not accept your company for two waltzes."

He concluded the conversation rapidly and took his leave, pleased with his progress.

Sharisse's thoughts went back to Andrew the minute the man was gone. She couldn't accept an offer from him because he would have a decided disgust of her when he found out her circumstances. She'd rather have no husband and live in poverty than perpetrate such a fraud upon him. She sighed as if the weight of the world were on her shoulders.

She imagined that she would have to go to the bank and withdraw a good deal of money, possibly several times. After all, Critchfield had said firmly that any moneys that she drew for her needs would not be counted or recalled if anything happened to Sidney. With that thought in mind, she ordered the phaeton.

While she was waiting, a letter came from Margaret. She scanned the crossed and recrossed lines, gathering that Margaret had her hands full with her heavy-handed mother prefacing every remark by, "Lady Satterleigh would like."

Margaret conveyed that she was having trouble inventing enough jobs to keep her mother busy and out of everyone's way. Sharisse was pleased with the thought and smiled.

Sharisse descended the steps when the phaeton was at the door, allowing the groom to assist her into the vehicle. The ride was short, but Sharisse was impatient to get the disagreeable task over with. She entered the bank, assuming her most formal manner.

"Miss Sharisse, it's been some time since we've seen you. What may we do for you today?" The old teller pulled his forelock in deference to her.

"I came to make a large withdrawal." She followed her own advice and didn't offer any explanation.

When the papers were signed and she had placed the bundle of bills in her large reticule, she thanked the bankers for their time and bid them good day. There were questions hanging in the air behind her, but no one dared question her, for she was trustee of the estate in her brother's absence.

Polly returned from the walk about the park, having made a decision. "Flynn, do you think that you could deliver a message to Lord Brookfield for me?"

"I ken do anythin' you need, missy."

Polly led the way to the writing desk and dashed off a note. "Take this, please, and wait for an answer. It's important."

"Don't you worrit yourself. Flynn will take of this fer ye." He clutched the paper. "Ye're sure ye don't want 'is nibs to stretch 'is length. I'd dearly love ta give him a taste of me fives."

"Oh, I wish that you could." She stared, fascinated, at the

wildly waving fist. "No, we can't always do what would give us pleasure."

Flynn looked crestfallen but obediently left the house, muttering under his breath.

Within a few minutes he was back and found Polly in the study with her sister reading out loud from a history book.

Flynn stood waiting for an opening. "Miss Polly, iffen ye want ta walk Lannie, I'll be that glad ta take ye."

Polly's face lit up like a hot fire on a cold morning. "Thank you. Lannie is most anxious to go."

Sharisse frowned slightly. "I thought you just took him out." She saw the glint of mischief in her sister's eye.

"Oh, I started to, but I thought it might be better if I waited until after we finished our reading. Then I would have something to look forward to."

This ingenious speech made Sharisse laugh. "Be off with you, then. You've done a fine job here. Soon I'll have to see about getting you a tutor. You have quite a thirst for knowledge." She only hoped that the money they would have to live on would support hiring a tutor.

"No one will bother little miss. I'll go bail ta that," Flynn offered as Polly jumped up.

Sharisse saw the procession off and then sat down to read the paper. She was again drawn to the cartoons. After seeing one that poked fun at one of the dukes, she laid it aside and contemplated her future. How she wished that Sidney were alive and that this course of action weren't necessary.

She closed her eyes and immediately a vision of Sidney sprang into her mind. He was bleeding profusely but he was breathing. She was so startled, she jumped out of her chair and started to pace about the room.

"My mind must be playing tricks on me." She shook her head and settled herself back into the chair. "I must be getting senile. I thought only older souls had such wishful dreams." She sighed and set out to make herself busy.

Gaining the safety of her room, she took out her feather-trimmed summer pelisse and contemplated the relative merits of sewing the money into the edges. The feathers were bulky anyway and, since she hardly ever wore the garment, no one need notice a thing.

"Flynn, did Lord Brookfield say he would meet us at Hyde Park?"

"Yes, Miss Polly, and he suggested that we meet him by the east gardens."

"Did he say that he'd be here directly?"

"That 'e did." He smiled fondly at the little girl.

"I have something very private to talk to him about. Will you take Lannie and walk a little ahead while we talk?"

The man nodded understandingly. It was clear she had won a place in his heart.

Andrew rounded the corner at a spanking pace, drawing the curricle to a plunging stop. "Flynn, would you be so kind as to walk the dog while I entertain Polly for a few minutes?"

Flynn obliged after helping Polly up into the carriage seat.

"Now, young lady," Andrew began, as they trotted along the carriageway, "tell me what this is about. I gather you're in some kind of trouble that you don't want Sharisse to know about."

"The trouble is really not so much mine as it is my sister's."

"Go on, Polly. You have my attention."

"It's Sir Vincent. You said that if ever I needed help I should come to you." She got the words out with a rush.

Andrew eyed her sharply, but waited for the rest of her disclosure.

"He is afraid of my Lannie."

That brought a shout of laughter to Andrew's lips. "How fortunate."

"Lannie doesn't like him and neither do I so I set the dog to scare him off. Now he won't come into the house if he thinks there's the least chance of Lannie being about." She seemed quite pleased with the arrangement.

"I can't imagine that Sir Vincent would be afraid of a dog that lolls his tongue and wags his tail."

"But he has such a beautiful set of teeth and they snap so loudly. His growl is quite menacing too." Polly treated him to her angelic smile.

"You little scamp! How did this get Sharisse into a fix?"

"Well, Sir Vincent thinks we're wealthy, because I put that rumor about to help her find a husband and now he has the intention of marrying her."

"The devil he has! Sorry, Polly. Go on." A muscle twitched angrily in his cheek.

"Wait until you hear the rest of it. He is trying to blackmail me into getting Sharisse to marry him. He said that if I don't convince her, he'll tell everyone that Sharisse stole his ring."

Andrew was having a great deal of difficulty holding his temper. "Is that all of it?"

"No. He said that he'd hidden the ring in Satterleigh House and that if Sharisse doesn't accept his offer of marriage tomorrow at the ball, he'll disclose the entire story and Sharisse will have to stand trial." A single tear escaped down one cheek.

"Polly, sweetheart, don't cry. I won't let anyone, ever, hurt you or Sharisse. You did right coming to me. I can handle this."

"What can you do?" she sniffed pitifully.

"First of all, no one is going to marry Sharisse but me. I hope you don't object to that, but even if you do, you are going to have me for a brother."

She nodded and sighed her relief.

"No objections from you?"

She shook her head. "I decided that of all the gentlemen that have come, you are the only one to be interested in Sharisse for herself. You never betrayed me to Sharisse and you seem to always be around to help."

"Thank you for the vote of confidence. Now do you think that you can keep this a secret between us?"

Polly nodded excitedly. "I love secrets."

"You must promise not to tell anyone about my intention to marry Sharisse or the threats Sir Vincent issued to you. In return, I'll fix Sir Vincent so that he won't be a threat to anyone again."

"I promise!" crooned Polly happily.

"We must conduct a search of the house without Sharisse's knowledge. Can you help?"

"If Sharisse is home I'll invent an errand, and if she's away, I'll stand guard." Polly was delighted in getting to help.

"We'll have Flynn help me. I suppose you've already guessed he's actually in my employ? I sent him over to be certain that you and your sister had some protection."

"I love Flynn, Andrew." The little girl's eyes were full of trust and love.

Polly was wreathed in smiles as she took Lannie's leash after stepping down from Andrew's carriage. "We'll see you in a few minutes," she reminded him.

Flynn mumbled to himself about the ways of the quality. "Miss Polly, remember that if ye need someone milled down, I'm yer man."

"Oh, Flynn, the opportunity might just come." Her laughter rang out as she pictured Sir Vincent. She skipped most of the way home and called for Sharisse upon entering.

Sharisse was out and Polly and Lannie took up their vigil on the staircase. She waited patiently to see what the results of the search were, but neither man would tell her what he found.

Polly was a mass of excitement as she made her way to bed that evening. The morrow would bring the resolution of her problem.

CHAPTER SEVENTEEN

Andrew's traveling carriage arrived promptly at seven, the team still fresh and eager to be off. He jumped out of the shiny new vehicle and handed his beaver top hat and gloves to Simms, who was waiting for him at the door. A fawn evening coat was molded superbly to his broad shoulders and cream satin knee breeches and small clothes completed the ensemble.

Sharisse floated down the wide staircase with ease in her primrose gown of sarcenet and lace. The hemline was draped with small bows holding the overskirt up so that the lighter shade of the underskirt showed. Her hair was drawn back from her face and from a loose knot hung several bouncing curls. A strand of pearls completed the toilette admirably, but when Andrew didn't say anything, Sharisse demanded, "You don't like what you see?"

"Now, darling, don't be totty-headed. Your mirror must tell you how stunning you are."

"Why is it then that I must prod you to make me a compliment." She teased him lightly.

"You'll have to take me in hand," he teased.

"Let's not be at dagger points. Cry truce and mayhap we can enjoy a pleasant evening." If he made too many comments in that vein she would be undone.

Andrew handed her into the plush interior of the coach. "Will it do? I bought it with you in mind."

"I thought we agreed to put aside our differences of opinion for the evening?" she countered.

"You asked, but I didn't agree," came the swift reply.

"In other words, you always do as you like? I certainly wouldn't be happy with that manner of order."

"What would you have of me, then? A tame lapdog that jumped at your slightest command? I promise you that you'd have contempt for that sort of creature within a fortnight."

Sharisse considered the justness of his argument and found she had nothing to say.

"Let me put your mind to rest. I promise to be as understanding as you'll allow, but firm enough to let you know I won't be circumvented."

Lady Englethorpe was waiting for them. "So this is the young lady who is making you dance to her tune!" She tapped Sharisse with her ornate fan.

Sharisse blushed deeply, her hand raised in protest, but Andrew cut her off.

"My dear aunt, you are so astute." He grinned engagingly at his relative and parried her humor with a bit of his own.

"Come along you two and we'll sit down to dinner. I want to have the pleasure of introducing Sharisse to your staid and proper Uncle Matthew.

Sharisse grew suddenly apprehensive. Andrew hadn't warned her that the dinner would be a family gathering. She suspected that the occasion had been created to put the family's collective seal of approval on the possible match.

Andrew whispered in her ear. "Don't worry, darling. I won't let them eat you. If they can approve me after what I have on my plate, surely yours can't be too full."

Sharisse gave a weak laugh. This was too much. She would never live down the consequences of her actions. She fought valiantly with the urge to turn tail and run. Sidney would have scoffed at such a course and she resolved to get through the evening. Get over the hard ground fastest had been her family motto and she saw no reason to argue or prolong the interview.

She parried questions with agility and found she enjoyed the verbal sparring. Uncle Matthew turned out to love a good horse and Sharisse was familiar with most of the studs in the area. She held her own while they spoke of breeding lines.

Andrew cut the conversation short when it turned to Sidney and apologized for leaving the assemblage. He gave a lame excuse that none of them believed, although they were too well bred to question it, and whisked Sharisse from the room.

Taking her for a tour of the house, he praised her handling of his numerous relatives. "You have the makings of a great political hostess, Sharisse, with your skill to change the subject of conversation and your ability to sum up situations. I make you my compliments."

Sharisse smiled warmly. "They aren't such a bad lot, once you get to know them, but the first few minutes, it was touch and go."

When it was time to repair to the ballroom, Andrew secured cards for them and indiscriminately wrote his name across half the dances.

"This isn't done, Andrew. You'll have me the talk of the town."

"Mayhap I ought to take up the entire program just to keep the young bucks at a distance."

Sharisse protested faintly but, afraid that he would carry out his threat, allowed him to return the card unchanged.

After the musicians finished tuning up, he led her proudly to the center of the floor to open the dancing. Sharisse was well aware that there were several ladies of greater consequence present and that Andrew, for courtesy's sake, should have asked to begin the festivities. Still it was comforting to know that he was interested to such a degree. She would let the matter slide until she had the cash amassed to make her permanent departure. Then she must put a stop to his courtship. Until then, she would enjoy his company to the utmost. But would she be able to walk away when the time came, a voice kept nagging at her.

"May I have a dance?" queried Sir Vincent at the conclusion of the first set. He took her card and examined it, raising his eyebrows in consternation. "Is this wise, my dear?"

Sharisse sent a pleading look at Andrew, but he merely smiled agreeably.

"I believe that I have an announcement to make later on," growled Sir Vincent threateningly.

Sharisse looked askance first at Sir Vincent, then at Andrew. "I'm afraid I haven't the vaguest clue to what you're speaking about."

Andrew cut in smoothly, "We'll have our own announcement to make shortly. Why don't you postpone yours until you can be certain that you'll get the results you expect?"

Sir Vincent's face took on a murderous look as he scratched his name on the card, but he managed to bow and turn away without a word.

"I don't think the gentleman—and I use the word in its loosest sense—is pleased. Perhaps a bit of rusticating on the Continent would be beneficial to the man."

"Andrew, could you arrange that?"

"Without a doubt, my darling. I have my ways, but enough of that. I see several young men queuing up to secure dances with you and I must not yet grow impatient." He bowed and wandered off in search of his aunt.

Sir Vincent claimed her later on for a waltz and almost as soon as the musicians had struck up the melody, he queried urgently, "Has your sister spoken to you?"

"My sister talks to me incessantly. Did you have something special on your mind?"

"Yes. Did she mention me in any way?"

"For some reason Polly has taken you in distinct aversion."

His lips pursed and his eyes narrowed as he contemplated his last option. His face showed the desperation of a man about to bet his last guinea.

"If you don't consent to be my bride this evening, I'm going to tell the entire assemblage that I have proof that you are the one that stole my ruby ring."

"I believe my credit will stand such an accusation, Sir Vincent. It would take more than an idle threat to make me bow to your wishes." Her voice held a great deal of distaste.

"Well then, how will you feel when I call the runners to Satterleigh House and they find the ring I planted there? Think of Polly and what would happen to her if you are transported."

Sharisse blanched and her stomach began to heave. "And exactly what is the price for your silence?"

"That you become my bride quite soon. I have pressing bills that require my immediate attention."

"You gazetted fortune hunter! Andrew said as much, but I thought his words a little strong. Now I see he was being quite kind."

Sir Vincent's face mottled with anger. His hold on her tensed and, for a moment, they lost time with the music. "I suggest that you think over my last offer quite seriously. At intermission I'm going to make my announcement. It's your choice which one it is." He curled his lip in a sardonic grin and began to chuckle as he noted Sharisse's discomfort.

As the dance finished, Andrew walked up to claim Sharisse and seemed to stumble.

"You clumsy oaf!" Sir Vincent muttered angrily.

"My apologies, Sir Vincent. I must have slipped on something on the floor." Andrew was profuse in his apologies and then promptly removed Sharisse from the scene.

Sharisse was left to ponder the circumstance of Andrew's supposed fall, but Sir Vincent's words forced her attention.

Andrew growled, "What did he say to make you so angry, darling? I promise that he won't have that power for long. I plan on settling his budget quite soon."

"I wish that I believed that you could mop his plate clean immediately. I'd like to applaud while you do it," she added feelingly. She allowed Andrew to lead her back to her next partner.

"I believe that can be arranged. Don't worry," he ordered her in an urgent whisper. "I know about his schemes and you'll find that he won't get very far with them."

Sharisse turned troubled eyes to his. "Are you certain you know the extent of them?

"My darling, trust me. I will set the matter to rights, I promise you."

She gave him a tremulous smile and when her next partner arrived, she allowed him to escort her into one of the sets.

Andrew watched as she was handed from partner to partner and periodically consulted his watch.

At intermission Sir Vincent strode purposefully to Sharisse and put a hand under her arm. "Well?"

Sharisse removed his hand like a piece of lint. "I suggest that you do your worst. I'll have nothing to do with the likes of you." If she had to flee the country, she would take Polly and be gone within the hour. She had most of their important things packed anyway.

Sir Vincent mounted the dais and called for everyone's attention. "My friends, I have a very important announcement to make. As you know, I lost a very valuable ring last week and I have finally tracked it down."

The man didn't get any farther, for Andrew was there beside him tromping hard on his toe. "Let me help, Sir Vincent. My friend here is a bit bashful about admitting he's made an error. The valuable ruby ring he's been telling us he thought was stolen has been found. It was in the pocket of the coat he's now wearing."

Sir Vincent looked stunned and involuntarily his hand went to both pockets of his coat and he pulled out the ring in question. Giving Andrew a thunderous scowl, he made the best of the event and raised the ring.

The crowd began to clap and Sir Vincent was left with no recourse except to bow and depart.

Andrew put himself in his path and escorted him from the room. "If I ever catch you within shouting distance of Sharisse again, I'll kill you without compunction. And the promise goes double for Polly. You are worse than the scum of the earth. Moreover, I think that a prolonged sojourn on the Continent is just what you need."

Sir Vincent knew he was beaten and merely withdrew, a broken man.

"Dear Aunt, have you seen Miss Satterleigh?"

His aunt looked up at him, raising her lorgnette to view him better. This one gesture had been known to quell many of the upper crust, but Andrew stood his ground.

"This is a first for you, Andrew. The young lady doesn't seem to dance to your piping at all—it's good for you, my boy. I believe that I'd try the east hall if you want to interrupt a tête-à-tête. She had a young buck following her as she left."

Andrew growled his thanks and set off with murder in his eye.

Sharisse had just descended the back stairs after repairing a torn flounce, when she was met by a pleading young man.

"Miss Satterleigh, I've been trying to get a word alone with you for ages, but someone is always cutting me out."

"Lieutenant Sutton, I don't believe that we have anything of a private nature to say."

The young man looked about, seeming to decide that he might not get another moment and flung himself to his knees. "Miss Satterleigh, I offer you my hand and heart in marriage."

Sharisse stood aghast at such an unprecedented occurrence. "Lieutenant Sutton, please get off your knees. Someone might see you." She looked about in embarrassment. "Conversation of this nature is repugnant to me."

The young soldier was beyond hearing her protests and went on praising her virtues despite Sharisse's protests until Andrew came upon them.

He jerked Lieutenant Sutton up and shook him. "Didn't you hear the lady? Be off, you young puppy," he ordered angrily, thrusting him in the direction of the ballroom.

"Let's play truant for a few minutes and have a turn about the garden."

Sharisse acquiesced, knowing her face was flushed with mortification at being caught in such a compromising situation and not knowing how to deal with Andrew's handling of both unpleasant situations.

She noted the strain about his mouth and thought it unusual. "I appreciate what you did with Sir Vincent. I don't quite know how you found his ring, but I had faith that you would come up with something plausible."

"You trusted me, you mean." A satisfied expression settled about his face.

"Yes, I suppose that I've trusted you for quite some time."

"Why, then, can't you tell me what's bothering you lately?"

"It's a family matter that I can't reveal."

"I want to become part of your family quite soon, my darling." He smiled warmly at her and stepped closer.

"This is so sudden, Andrew," she responded, desperately trying to buy some time.

"My darling, I've been hinting broadly for weeks about the fact that I intend to make you my wife." His eyes softened and he chafe her hand tenderly before kissing it.

"I suspected as much, but I find that I cannot accept your suit, however advantageous it may be." She said the words as boldly as she could, her heart crying at the thought of losing him.

"Don't you think that you could find it in your heart to accept me as a husband and lover?" His voice held a deal of pain.

"It's not that, Andrew. It's just that there are circumstances that I can't control or explain and because of them, I can not marry you."

"You admit that you love me, then?" he prodded gently.

She nodded, not daring to speak with the large lump forming in her throat.

"Very well, then, I accept your decision." His voice was tinged with something that Sharisse couldn't quite identify.

Sharisse gasped. She hadn't expected him to capitulate so easily but she managed a wan smile at his acceptance of her decision.

"Even if you can't marry me, could you go for a drive with me tomorrow morning? I believe that the weather will be exceptional and we'll have a picnic."

Sharisse hesitated, thinking that each time she was with him, she found herself tumbling farther into love.

"You're not going to try to change my mind about marrying you?" she inquired suspiciously.

"I wouldn't dream of it."

He had a particularly wicked gleam in his eye that made Sharisse uncomfortable, but she swallowed her objections and changed the subject. "What time will you be arriving tomorrow?"

"Would nine be too early?"

"Yes, I have some important business early and I think it might be better if we set the time for eleven."

He seemed to do some quick calculating and then returned, "I'll split the difference with you. Ten o'clock is my best offer."

"I'll be ready. You know I love picnics."

CHAPTER EIGHTEEN

Sharisse had just completed her next withdrawal in the comfort of one of the bank's offices when she heard Andrew's voice. His laugh was unmistakable.

"I plan on going in comfort," he joked good-naturedly.

"With that amount, my lord, the king could go in comfort."

"But, Ashton, I believe in being prepared for any contingency."

Sharisse wondered what the large amount of money was for and where he was planning on going? Her heart sank. It was one thing to end the relationship, but for him to go away without a word to her, well, she hoped it wouldn't come to that. The words "prepared for any contingency" bothered her. She couldn't imagine Andrew not being prepared in any situation. Look at the way he had handled Sir Vincent and young Sutton. He was forever giving Polly secret looks lately that made her believe that he'd rescued Polly from some consequence.

She sighed. To be able to place the entire mess in his lap and have him solve it was tempting, but she couldn't take the chance on seeing his love turn to contempt. Anything was preferable to that.

She finished tying her bonnet with the utmost care, stalling for time so that she could be certain that he had gone before she ventured back into the main room of the bank.

When she finally escaped into the warm morning air, she knew it behooved her to hurry. Andrew was due to pick her up in a very few minutes and he had a head start. As she let the groom thread the streets, her mind wandered back to Andrew. If he pushed her quite hard, she knew that she couldn't stand firm against his suit, loving him to distraction as she did, and so she tried valiantly to discover a way to have this last treat without putting temptation in her way.

A solution finally hit her and she began to laugh. Andrew would be fairly flummoxed. She was still chuckling when she hurried into the house. "Polly, Robbie! I must speak with you right away."

"Was there something that you wanted, dear?" The old woman's voice held a great deal of affection for Sharisse.

"Yes, indeed. We have all been invited to go on a picnic with Lord Brookfield and he will be arriving any minute. Do you think you can be ready?"

Polly's face beamed her approval of the plan. "Wonderful. Can I bring Lannie?"

Sharisse grinned. "Not this time, Polly, though I'd love to see Andrew's face."

When Andrew arrived a short while later, Polly darted into the front hall to meet him. "Thank you for inviting us to go along on your outing. I love a picnic. Sharisse said that you wouldn't want Lannie but I thought I'd ask just the same."

"Oh, I see Polly put her case before I could speak with you," said Sharisse grinning.

Andrew swallowed heavily, looked heavenward, and then began to laugh. "My darling Sharisse, you never cease to surprise me."

"I knew you couldn't be so poor-spirited as to make Polly and Miss Roberts miss such a fine afternoon."

His mouth twitched. "Indeed not. I hope we aren't going to be crowded.

"Oh," moaned Sharisse distractedly, "didn't you bring the traveling carriage? I was certain that you would."

"Yes, my darling, I brought the traveling carriage and a team instead of a mere pair. You are all welcome, but I suggest that you ladies each take a warm pelisse, as you may be cold before the day is over."

"Polly, I believe that Lannie wouldn't like being cooped up in the coach for such a long time and it wouldn't be fair to Miss

Roberts or your sister to constantly have the dog on their laps. You understand, don't you?" He bent down to the child as he spoke.

"Yes, Andrew, but he'll be lonely while we're gone."

"We'll give him a special treat when we return."

Polly's eyes shone with anticipation and Sharisse found she had a large lump in her throat. Andrew would make an admirable guardian for her.

Miss Roberts agreed. "I think your young man has a deal of sense, Sharisse. Don't let him go."

Sharisse didn't know quite where to look. Robbie had never been more plain-spoken.

Lord Brookfield murmured appreciatively, "Thank you for the kind words. I'll see that she keeps them in mind."

Sharisse's spine prickled with apprehension and she cast about for further protection from his advances. Seeing Flynn passing in the back hall, she beamed her satisfaction. "Lord Brookfield, I believe that it might be a good idea to take Flynn with us. The man has a special knack with Polly and he would be just the trump we need if we're accosted by . . . highwaymen. Would you mind?"

Andrew threw Polly a questioning look, but she merely shook her head no. Only then did Andrew permit himself to grin. "As you wish, my darling." Finally he couldn't contain his mirth and he began to laugh.

Sharisse smiled with satisfaction at having foiled his plans to get her alone and hurried to her bedchamber. She didn't care to leave the reticule with her money in it unattended, nor did she have time to find a safe place for it, so she brought it along with her pelisse after placing several handkerchiefs and toiletries on top of it to disguise the bulk.

Soon they were on the post road, bowling along at a brisk pace. The carriage was admirably sprung and even Miss Roberts commented on how comfortable it was. They kept to the post road for almost two hours and Sharisse began to wonder where he was taking them. The fact that Andrew had withdrawn a great deal of money from the bank that morning seemed to suddenly have great significance. It was just that Sharisse couldn't quite catch what it was.

"Andrew, isn't it about time we found a suitable place where we can stop?"

"Your wish is my command." Within minutes he had drawn up on a grassy spot, the river flowing nearby.

The coachman saw to the horses while Flynn pulled a huge hamper from the front seat along with a large blanket. He spread it on the grass and placed the hamper on it. Andrew invited Sharisse to see to its contents.

Her host seemed in the best of moods as the meal progressed and every once in a while a broad smile crossed his face. The look made Sharisse more than curious and she surmised that he was up to something.

Sharisse packed carefully away the leftovers. As she folded and wrapped, she wondered why he had chosen to go so far along the post road to stop at a very ordinary picnic spot. When the coach resumed its journey in the same direction Sharisse's suspicions were aroused in earnest. "Andrew, where are you taking us?"

He looked down at her, twin devils jumping in his eyes. "Why, my darling, I'm kidnapping you."

For several seconds silence reigned and then Sharisse began to laugh. "Andrew, you infuriating jokester, where are we headed?"

"To Dover, where, if we hurry, I hope to catch the packet to France. I plan for us to be married at the English Embassy there and have our honeymoon in Paris."

Sharisse digested this. "I thought you accepted my refusal to marry you and I haven't changed my mind."

"You don't consent to a kidnapping, darling. You consent to an elopement. There's a vast difference."

Polly snickered and Miss Roberts sighed contentedly.

"What about Miss Roberts and Polly? Did you plan on kidnapping them too?" She began to see the humor of the situation.

"No, indeed." He went on in a philosophical tone, "But

then, when did you ever do anything by the book? It is one of the things I like best about you."

"I hope that you don't change your mind, now that the die seems to be cast."

"Nothing in this world could make me change my mind, my adorable vixen."

Sharisse studied him speculatively for a moment and then straightened her shoulders and thrust her chin forward. "You might as well know, then, that my brother died in India and the property is entailed. That makes me just as much a fortune hunter as Sir Vincent."

"Sweetheart, I've known from the day I met you about Sidney and I've seen your heroic efforts to try to provide for Polly and yourself. I told you long ago that I won't cast stones. I just wish that I could have gotten you to confide in me sooner."

"Andrew, I've been such a fool." She allowed herself to be pulled into his arms and kissed.

When he set her back, he turned to Miss Roberts. "I trust that you have no objections?"

"Who am I to interfere with the face of love?" Miss Roberts busied herself looking out the window at the scenery.

"And you, Polly, how do you feel about this?" Sharisse inquired anxiously.

"I've decided that he's a trump." To Sharisse she leaned forward and whispered, "And more than that, he won't let you down when you're in trouble."

Andrew chortled while Sharisse grinned. They lost themselves in touching hands and sharing speaking glances for a few minutes until Miss Roberts gasped.

Polly hung out the window to see that they were drawing up to the wharves and that there was a carriage with a crest emblazoned on the side that she recognized instantly. "Margaret!"

Sharisse came back to the present with a thud. "Polly, what's gotten into you?" She pulled briskly on her little sister's skirts and hauled her back into the carriage.

"It seems, my love, that your family has also arrived in Dover, but for what reason I daren't guess."

Sharisse's view confirmed that not only Margaret but her mother and nurse were all at dockside. She pushed the carriage door open and strode over to her sister-in-law. "What on earth are you doing here, Margaret, four weeks from your lying in? You ought to be home resting up for your ordeal," she scolded the girl gently.

"Indeed! That's exactly what I said. Only four weeks until confinement and with this jolting, she could lose the baby." Albinia's acid voice was piercing but her daughter paid her no mind.

"It's Sidney. He's due in right now on the *Star of India.*" She pointed to where the passengers were disembarking in a streaming throng. "Isn't it wonderful? They say he's been wounded in the head and arm but that he's going to be fine. I don't understand why he's coming from India and not France, but it makes no difference. I'm so excited."

Sharisse drew a long steady breath to help her assimilate the information.

Andrew had walked up to hear the last of the conversation and shared a triumphant smile with Sharisse. She blushed and grinned and then laughed.

Andrew whispered in her ear. "It seems that your prediction about Sidney's prognosis has won the day, love. Mayhap I'll hire you out as a fortune-teller. We could make a great deal of money."

Sharisse whispered back, "You don't need any more money and I find the fortune-telling business is just too taxing." She grinned.

"Just so," he agreed readily. "You must conserve your strength for other more important concerns," he murmured with a grin.

When finally there seemed no one left, Margaret's face began to crumple and with it her back started to sag. She began to rub it.

Andrew wiped a spot of dirt off Lady Satterleigh's face and

consoled her. "It is quite possible that he may have missed the ship and will be in on the next one in about six weeks."

"Sidney!" she cried at that moment, seeing the man with his arm in a sling and a heavy bandage on his head.

He waved with his good arm and rushed down the gangplank to catch her in his arms. Sidney hugged her fiercely, as close as the obstruction between them would permit. He turned to speak with the rest but was cut off.

"She shouldn't be here with only four weeks until the happy event. It wasn't safe to travel," Albinia complained bitterly.

Nurse was helping Margaret with rubbing her back, and the girl's face was drawn.

Sidney surveyed the waiting group. "Thank you all for coming to see me home, but there was not the slightest necessity for such a family gathering. I'd far rather you'd taken more care of my wife." His tone was slightly acerbic and he looked apprehensively at Margaret before continuing. "Whose idea was this?"

Andrew volunteered freely. "Sharisse and I didn't come to see you home, though we're certainly glad you're here. We didn't have the foggiest notion that you might be here today."

"Then why are you here?" puzzled Sidney.

Sharisse grinned but remained silent. It was Polly that jumped in with an explanation.

"Andrew's kidnapping Sharisse. He's taking her to France to marry her and we're going along." The little girl seemed quite pleased with the arrangement.

Albinia shrieked her outrage, while nurse merely clucked.

"Andrew, I think you must be short of a sheet if you are planning to elope with such redoubtable chaperones."

"I beg you to believe that it was not in my plans. Your sister added the extra ingredients without my knowledge and I found that I didn't care to let a little problem stop me. Now that you're home, I'm informing you of my intent to marry your sister with or without your consent."

"You have my blessing and I think that you're just the man to handle her, but why go to Paris to be married? We'd like to witness this event." He then looked down at his wife tenderly and she agreed. "I think we ought to get the ceremony over quickly, so I can get my wife back home where she belongs."

It didn't take Andrew long to locate the local bishop, and the two carriages pulled up in front of the rectory.

A young curate answered the door, amazed at the number of members of the quality who were on his doorstep. "May I be of assistance to you, my children?"

Andrew moved forward. "We would like to see the bishop. We would like to have a wedding performed."

The curate moved to one side, motioning the group into the small hall while he picked up the skirts of his cassock and ran up the stairs. Sidney pulled out a chair for his wife, but it was Andrew who had to assist her into it.

Mrs. Moffat proceeded to list her grievances to no one in particular, because the entire assemblage seemed to have turned a deaf ear. Nurse kept up her chatter and massaged Margaret's back, while Margaret merely closed her eyes and rested her head on her husband's good arm.

Polly skipped about the room, peering into every nook and cranny, while Miss Roberts tried in vain to subdue her.

Sharisse's eyes locked with Andrew's and she wondered how she could have been so silly as to almost throw away the best chance of happiness she would ever have.

The curate was back shortly, followed with slow dignity by the bishop, a very rotund man whose girth proclaimed his appetite.

"I understand that you wish to be married," he stated briefly to Andrew.

"That's correct, Your Worship." Andrew stood a little straighter as he spoke.

"Very well, please come into my parlor." The modest room was nicely furnished, showing the man either had an ample income or that he spent it well.

Everyone gathered around. Andrew explained to the bishop that they required a special license as they had been going to be married in France but that he was willing to stand the expense.

Before the bishop could answer, Margaret gave a slight cry and started to collapse. Andrew was at her side and caught her to him, then found her a comfortable chair.

Nurse's eyes were snapping. "Are you all right, baby?" She mopped Margaret's brow with lavender water.

Sidney stood beside his wife while Andrew came forward to the bishop again.

"You see, Bishop, we find ourselves in something of an emergency."

The bishop looked him up and down and then over at Margaret. "Yes, but I believe that you've left it until almost too late. Well, we'll see that the baby has a name." He picked up the Bible from his curate and opened it and motioned Andrew to stand beside Margaret.

Andrew's face registered total shock and his eyes flew heavenward before he succumbed to uproarious laughter. "Sir, this is not the lady I wish to marry."

The bishop's cherubic face took on a dark look. "This is too much, this poor soul in this condition and you want to marry another?"

Sharisse and Polly began to giggle, while Sidney drew himself up to his full height and roared, "I'll have you know that this lady is my wife." He put his arm possessively around Margaret, who was having difficulty breathing.

Sharisse murmured to Polly, "I believe that we've just set a new precedent for weddings."

"Yes," agreed Polly readily, "everyone is a candidate for bedlam."

Andrew regained some sense of expediency and pulled Sharisse to him, inquiring politely, "May we begin now?"

The bishop shook his head in disapproval but started reading the marriage vows. Sharisse watched Andrew's face, as he scrutinized hers and they gave firm answers to the man's questions.

The bishop had almost finished reading, "I now pronounce . . ." when Margaret doubled over with a shattering groan.

Nurse stood up muttering, "I kept trying ta tell ye that the baby is coming now, but no one wanted ta listen."

"Where's the bedroom?" barked Sidney and began issuing orders to the clergymen.

At the same time a clamor broke loose from the rest of the occupants of the room. Mrs. Moffat was busily giving her stock-in-trade "I told you so," while Polly kept asking Sharisse what all the fuss was about.

Andrew was the only silent one in the room and merely picked Margaret up and took her up the stairs to the indicated room.

"Sidney, don't worry too much," Sharisse soothed. "Women have babies all the time and nurse has delivered her share."

When Margaret was settled, Andrew turned to Sidney. "This must be caused by the bumping of the carriage along the way."

Sidney eyed his friend with a wry smile. "No, it's just that my dearly beloved wife can't count. She has no head for figures. That's why I was so surprised to see her and wanted to get your wedding over as quickly as possible."

That comment elicited a quick response. "Yes, Bishop, please finish the ceremony. I want nothing to stand in my way."

The poor man was in a quandary. A woman was giving birth in his bachelor house and the entire place had taken on the appearance of a tavern. "Ah, ah, ah, I now pronounce you man and wife. You may kiss the bride."

Andrew brushed Sharisse's lips lightly and they followed him downstairs to sign the register. While they were there, Margaret let out a piercing scream.

The harassed cleric groaned, "Dear Lord, what am I going to do?"

"We won't disturb your household for long. As soon as is possible we'll move Lady Satterleigh to the nearest hotel to recover, providing I can find a doctor to give his permission."

The curate spoke up. "I can run and get you Mr. Edwards. He's only two doors down." He was striding out the door as he spoke.

As Sidney descended the stair, his face ashen with fear, Andrew recommended, "Why don't you check out the hotels and secure a first-rate place for you and Lady Satterleigh? Polly could go with you."

Both men silently agreed it was best to remove Polly from the premise.

Sidney placed an arm about Polly and they went out together.

Polly stopped stock still as they entered the street area. Flynn was lounging at his ease, by the corner of the building, eyeing a gentleman with distaste. The elegant figure consulted his watch before descending from a spartan coach piled with baggage.

"Sir Vincent," she whispered angrily. "Sidney, I must tell Flynn something before we visit the hotel."

Sidney was reluctant, but seeing Polly's determination, allowed her to go.

"Flynn," she called urgently, "may I speak to you a minute?"

"Did ye want somethin', Miss Polly?"

"Yes," she stated baldly. "I just wanted to tell you that the time for Sir Vincent to receive his just reward has arrived."

"Ye want to see a little footwork?" Flynn grinned.

She looked over to where Sidney stood waiting impatiently. "No, I want him to have an accident. Do you think that you could manage to trip him or something?"

"I'll do my best," he promised as he set off across the street.

"What was that all about, Polly?" her brother inquired curiously.

"Let's just say, I'm evening the score."

"Polly, I don't like the sound of that. What did the man do to you?" His voice was stern.

Polly merely shrugged her shoulders and grinned. "He tried

to blackmail Sharisse and me but Andrew fixed it. I merely wanted to add my tuppence to the score."

Sidney's fist clenched and his lips compressed into a thin line. "It seems that I owe my new brother a debt of gratitude."

At that moment Flynn bowed to Sir Vincent and at the same time seemed to stumble, knocking the man into the watering trough. "Compliments of Miss Polly Satterleigh," he breathed quietly, silently begging the man to take a swing at him.

Polly and Sidney roared with laughter as they walked arm in arm into the hotel.

Sir Vincent was left to drip his way to the back stairs, muttering imprecations about small children.

Andrew reached into his pocket and pulled out his notecase and removed a couple of bills. Handing them to the bishop, he thanked the man profusely for his service.

At the sight of such largess the old man's eyes brightened considerably. His face lost its forbidding appearance and resolved itself again into the kindly image he liked to portray.

The curate came hurrying in with the doctor in tow. As he entered the room, nurse could be heard to shout, "I don't need any help."

A moment or two later the doctor reappeared. "As this is a first baby, it may be several hours before the child is born. I understand you wish to remove to a hotel. I believe that it will be safe if she is carried out to the carriage and carried to her room. There is an excellent establishment around the corner." With that he picked up his hat and moved toward the door. Again Andrew parted with some of his store.

As the doctor left, a young clerk from the Bellefontaine Hotel announced that Sir Sidney had a room ready for Lady Satterleigh.

Andrew made his way to the chamber where Margaret lay in pain. Within minutes he had directed the whole operation and was placing Margaret on the clean linen of the hotel bed.

Several hours later a squalling cry from above could be heard and the group heaved a collective sigh of relief. Polly came into the drawing room from the kitchen, a smirk written plainly on her face, to share in the news.

Mrs. Moffat came shuffling importantly down the stairs to Sidney. "You have a fine baby son."

"And my wife?"

"She is fine. She just needs her rest."

Sidney stood up to make his way to Margaret's bedchamber. Mrs. Moffat thrust herself in his way. "It's too soon to see her, she needs to rest."

"Out of my way, woman! Nothing in the world is going to prevent me from seeing my wife and son." He brushed aside his astonished mother-in-law and marched into the room.

Andrew turned to Sharisse. "I don't believe that Albinia will rule that household. Now that things are resolved here, my darling wife, I believe that it's time we try to catch the night packet."

"Just a few more minutes. I would like to speak to Sidney." She accompanied the request with a flutter of her eyelashes.

"Trying to turn me up sweet, already, my love?"

Sidney returned a few moments later and signaled that Mrs. Moffat could rejoin his wife. As they took turns congratulating Sidney, Andrew glanced at his timepiece and then held up a restraining hand. "I'm sure that no one will object at this time if I take my wife on her honeymoon?"

Polly hugged Sharisse quickly. "I almost wish that we hadn't met Sidney before we went. Now I miss a trip to Paris."

"Don't fret, little one," Andrew advised, grinning, "I'll see that you get there next year at the latest. Besides, if you're good while we're gone, we might find you a present or two."

Miss Roberts caught Polly to her and beamed her pleasure at the couple. "Take care of her, son."

"When we return, I expect that you and Polly will have your trunks packed and ready to move to Brookfield Hall. Sharisse tells me that she won't stay without you."

Miss Roberts merely nodded, wiping the mist from her eyes.

Andrew led his bride to dockside, the rest of the party,

following merrily in their wake. Polly had found a bit of rice in the hotel kitchen and was passing it out to everyone.

Flynn and the coachman were laden down with Lord Brookfield's valises, but good-naturedly took a handful of the rice.

Sidney dipped generously into the sack and tossed rice at the two as they gained the gangplank.

Andrew shielded Sharisse from the barrage and both laughed their way up the wooden boards. They turned at the rail to wave good-bye to their well-wishers while the two servants stowed their luggage. Sharisse was smiling happily at the crowd.

Polly called, "Will you bring me a new doll?"

"Only if you're a pattern-card young lady while we're gone."

Andrew advised Sidney, "Polly has a singularly unique treat in store for you at the Meadows—another new member to your family. What a distinctive heredity." He began to chuckle and Sharisse giggled.

"Sidney, you're going to love my new pet and it's not true that he's as big as a horse."

A startled expression crossed Sidney's face and he growled to Andrew, "Did you bring any animals home from India?"

Flynn and the coachman doffed the hats as they passed and Andrew stopped them to place a couple of coins in their hands. "Not I," he replied, still convulsed with laughter.

Sharisse paused to wipe her eyes, when she suddenly gasped with dismay.

Andrew gazed down at his bride to see what the trouble was, and Sharisse pointed to Sir Vincent, who was starting across the water.

Sharisse turned her face into his collar and whispered, "I don't wish to share our wedding voyage with the likes of him, but what can we do about it?"

Andrew grinned wickedly and murmured, "Depend on me." He left Sharisse with a wink and walked to the middle of the gangplank. "Sir Vincent, I believe that you mistook the day for your travel arrangements."

"I see you have stolen my thunder and married the heiress yourself," Sir Vincent sneered derisively, ignoring Andrew's remarks. "I hope that you realize the extent of the family you have aligned yourself with. I wish you joy of the entire lot." He spat the last words out.

"Sir Vincent, I take extreme exception to your remarks. I find the Satterleighs of fine lineage, far better bred than some I can speak of." He took a threatening step forward.

Sir Vincent backed up. "Your wife isn't any better than a high-priced doxy."

Andrew's face darkened. "I'm afraid you've gone your length."

Sir Vincent had barely time to assimilate the words and the expression on Lord Brookfield's face.

Andrew moved forward, stomping quite roughly on the old wooden planks.

Sir Vincent recoiled quickly, muttering obscenities on the vacillating qualities of females. As the planks wobbled, he lost his balance and tumbled head first into the harbor with a resounding splash.

Andrew raised his hands in a gesture of innocence, his face a study in feigned astonishment, and turned first to his wife and then to the group on the pier.

Sharisse began to shake with laughter. "Andrew, my long-suffering husband, that wasn't quite what I had in mind, but I assure you, I'm perfectly happy with the results."

He pulled her to him, waved the crowd a last farewell, and carried her into the captain's suite.

"How did you ever get the captain to part with his cabin?" Sharisse's voice was breathless and her heart began to flutter erratically.

He closed the distance between them, ravishing her lips with his own, holding her firmly against the hard length of him. When he heard her moan of surrender, he tilted her head back tenderly. "Every man has his price, sweetheart, and I found his without much trouble. The major question is, have I found yours?"

Sharisse peeked up at him through her fringe of lashes and murmured saucily, "No, but you're getting warm."

Several onlookers were pulling a sodden Sir Vincent from the cold waters as the vessel set sail.

Polly gave a satisfied giggle. "I think that the man is accident prone."

Flynn guffawed and slapped his knees in merriment.

Sidney observed dryly, "I believe that Sir Vincent has developed a recent affinity for water."